Alanna Knight

The Coffin Lane Murders

An Inspector Faro Mystery

MACMILLAN

First published 1998 by Macmillan

an imprint of Macmillan Publishers Ltd
25 Eccleston Place, London SW1W 9NF
and Basingstoke

Associated companies throughout the world

ISBN 0 333 68912 7

1 3 5 7 9 8 6 4 2

A CIP catalogue record for this book is available from
the British Library.

Phototypeset by Intype London Ltd
Printed by Mackays of Chatham plc, Chatham, Kent

To Pat and Bill McDonald
with love

Chapter One

The prelude to each major disaster in Detective Inspector Faro's personal life was a calm wherein all the untidy fragments, the small irritations that clouded every day, were forgotten. The world seemed to hold its breath, as if being alive in itself was a joy almost too great to bear, a burden of gratitude too great to express.

And so it was that Jeremy Faro was to remember for the rest of his life one afternoon in late December when he stood on the ice-packed road above Duddingston village and watched as the sunset came down like blood on the fast-frozen loch.

The eve of the first murder . . .

The great city of Edinburgh lay to his right. Behind a veil of mist the rose-tinted walls of the castle were the home of a fairy-tale princess, awaiting a knight on a white charger, while far below its steep battlements history's blood-soaked High Street and dark, foul-smelling closes arose from a shroud of innocent purity, temporarily absolved from all evil.

It had not snowed for several days but the fields that bordered Faro's home in Newington lay white and untrodden, like the pages of a story yet to be written. A dread story he had never dreamed he would ever have to tell.

Already hurtling past him between the snowdrifts on the narrow road through Queen's Park from the direction of the Palace of Holyroodhouse carriages crowded with young people headed towards the loch. Frozen solid for the past week, delighting all but the wildfowl cut off from their food supply, the loch was Edinburgh's favourite winter resort.

On its far side ran the 'Innocent Railway' (proudly so-called since no lives had been lost in its history). Originally it had been a single-track horse-drawn freight line between St Leonards and Musselburgh and a convenient method of transport for the Fisherrow fishwives. The advent of steam locomotion had made it a popular mode of transport with extra coaches for the convenience of fare-paying passengers. Now each scheduled train was crowded with skaters from Musselburgh and beyond.

Watching the energetic scene, Faro acknowledged the ghost of himself among the couples gracefully curving their ways across the ice. As a young man, only yesterday it seemed, courting Vince's mother, skating had offered daring opportunities for a man and a lass in love to hold each other close in the respectable name of maintaining balance.

He smiled wryly at the excited laughter, the distant shrieks of mirth from the loch, the lasses with their shy eagerness, the lads trying to impress with a show of strong manly reliability.

'Nothing ever really changes,' he muttered, addressing no one in particular and nodding in the direction of Craigmillar Castle's lofty ruin. People –

the bad and the good – were the same now as when sad Queen Mary, seeking respite from scheming nobles and a bitter marriage, had looked down on this scene from those eyeless windows. The only difference: justice was administered with more humanity, and death by the hangman's rope regarded as a more civilised exit than the torture chamber and executioner's block.

Shading his eyes against the luminous western sky, he looked towards the section of the loch occupied by older, more dignified groups, families with young children, ladies elegant in velvet fur-lined cloaks, bonnets and muffs, the gentlemen in top hats and greatcoats. The swirl of colour and laughter evoked a sigh of nostalgia from Faro.

He had given Vince his first skating lesson here. Dr Vince Laurie who was out there with his Olivia, now a doting husband and father of Jamie Beaumarcher Laurie, their handsome two-year-old son and the apple of Faro's eye.

Oh, life had been – still was – so good.

But where was wee Jamie? Panic touched Faro in a moment of unearthly foreboding as if a veil hiding the future had been wrenched aside. Why wasn't he with his parents?

Heart hammering, narrowing his eyes, he scanned the fast-moving groups.

A shout from the loch. A wave in his direction.

With a sigh of relief, he responded. Away from the main group, concealed by the skaters, Vince's partner Dr Conan Pursley and his wife Kate guided Jamie gently along between them. They moved less vigorously than Vince and Olivia, since Kate was recovering from one of the woman's troubles that plagued her. Not yet forty, Kate was invalidish and frail, her menstrual problems and miscarriages subjects fit only for behind-hand whispers anywhere but a doctor's surgery.

To be childless after ten years of marriage was the Pursleys' one inconsolable grief and Faro was sad for this unjust trick of fate upon a fine doctor like Conan Pursley, who had dedicated his whole life to campaigning against the cruelties inflicted on the mentally disturbed. Refusing to regard them as dangerous or beyond the pale of normal life, he considered most as merely sick of a foul disease for which doctors had not yet found a cure.

The Glasgow institution, where he had worked when approached by Vince directly but tactfully to join the practice, had been eager to give Dr Pursley a glowing reference and recommendation. Even if his theories regarding the nature of insanity were somewhat avant-garde and difficult to reconcile with medical beliefs and treatments which had changed little since the Middle Ages, his superiors had nothing but praise for this most caring of their doctors.

The two partners had soon become not just colleagues but close friends. Conan was the elder by ten years but their attitudes to life and society were similar and they shared a mutual devotion to golf. For that Vince was prepared to forgive Conan's unfortunate relationship by marriage to Sir Hedley Marsh and his wife's decision to live in Solomon's Tower and look after the 'Mad Bart', who was her uncle.

Vince had few secrets from Conan who knew that his partner's scorn for the aristocracy and everything they stood for was based on the abuse his mother had suffered early in her life. Despite the love that his stepfather Jeremy Faro had lavished upon him, Vince remained haunted by a past that no honour, no distinction or hard-won achievement could ever obliterate.

He was illegitimate, the result of the rape of a fourteen-year-old servant by an aristocratic house guest in a Highland castle, at one of the jolly huntin' shootin' parties that Sir Hedley liked to reminisce about.

Conan understood and sympathised. His father had been an estate factor. After bitter experiences of the gentry he had taken his family to Glasgow and set up a successful business as a landscape gardener.

William Pursley had early discovered his only son's extreme interest in natural history, namely the insects and small creatures that inhabit gardens. Accordingly, while their daughter went to work in a local merchant's mansion, they had scrimped and saved to put Conan through medical college.

Conan had met Kate during the summer vacation while working with his father, landscaping the gardens of an aristocratic mansion whose owner was intent on restoring its sixteenth-century features, particularly the Jacobite rose which had figured strongly in their family history.

The owner's only child, Kate, was irresistibly drawn to handsome Conan, seeing him as a humble but wildly attractive labourer from the class forbidden to one of her birth. Hopelessly in love, it was not until the day Conan asked her to marry him that he revealed the truth: 'Some day soon, I will be a doctor.

A very respectable profession and I hope to be able to support a wife.'

'The rest you know,' he told Vince. Kate was already an heiress and when Sir Hedley died, she stood to inherit Solomon's Tower. 'There won't be much money in that, for sure,' laughed Conan, for he had no longer any qualms about her wealth. 'If ever I have the temerity to mention it she assures me that my amount of brains makes us more than equal.'

Pausing, he waved to Faro, who stood watching them from the roadside above the loch.

Faro was a tall, slim man, in his late forties, his thick fair hair now threaded with grey, with fine-boned distinguished features. The dark blue eyes were remarkable for their intensity, so penetrating that it seemed that no man could ever tell a direct lie into them, eyes that saw deep down inside the speaker to where the well of truth lay hidden.

'Put a horned helmet on him and give him a shield and an axe to carry and he'd still look out of his time. As if he'd just stepped off a Viking raider's ship in the Firth of Forth,' said Conan, and as they sat down on a fallen tree trunk to remove their skates he regarded his friend curiously. It was difficult to imagine that Vince had once hated his policeman stepfather and there seemed so little difference in their ages that they might have passed as brothers.

Conan laughed. 'Considering his good looks and, begging your pardon, old chap, but he was still young when your mama died, and he's a virile man after all, why on earth did he never marry again? Not from any lack of opportunity, I'd reckon.'

Vince declined the cigar he offered. 'There were

one or two promising encounters. We had hopes regarding a childhood sweetheart in Orkney, then there was an actress – and a Grand Duchess. Most recently and, I suspect, best suited to him, although he would not agree, one of this new breed of women– '

'A suffragist, you mean.' Conan chuckled. 'Good Lord. I don't see him with a blue-stocking.'

Vince shook his head. 'This one was – is – a writer. He approves of such ladies in principle but not, alas, as a life partner. Or so he says.'

'What happened to her?'

'It's a long story. She went back to Ireland.'

'Ireland? That's not the ends of the earth. Why, Kate's family go there regularly for the shooting every year.'

Vince said nothing and, aware that no more confidences were forthcoming, Conan changed the subject.

'What was your mother like? I mean, is he still devoted to her memory?'

'I think so. And that he feels a powerful amount of guilt for neglecting her while she was alive.'

Conan frowned. 'Other women, you mean?'

'Not at all. He was completely faithful. Unless you could call the whole of Edinburgh City Police a rival. He always was – still is – passionately devoted to his work. Reading between the lines, I think that has always been his greatest problem where marrying again was concerned.' Vince sighed. 'He still takes flowers to her grave every week. But alas, I sometimes think that had she survived she would never have been able to keep up with his intellect.'

Aware of Conan's expression, he added anxiously, 'That's just my opinion; I'm not being disloyal. But remember my mother was still a child with little or no education when she had me. I was ten when they married and after those early skirmishes we've got along famously. We've seen each other through many a tight spot and I don't mean just in connection with crimes, although my medical knowledge has been of some help.

'I've watched him develop a taste for music, a love of books and good living. He's become a cultured – well – gentleman. Such attributes are regarded as unnecessary adornments and somewhat scorned in his profession, I can tell you.'

He shrugged uncomfortably under Conan's glance. 'Yes, the thought still niggles. If – if my mother's last baby hadn't killed her, what would their life have been like now?'

'True,' said Conan thoughtfully. 'Great passion dies and,' he added frankly, 'then one needs a partner to share one's intellectual pursuits.'

'I hope when Olivia and I have been married as long as you that we'll be as happy. You and Kate seem to have the ideal marriage – even without children.'

Conan considered for a moment before replying. 'Can't say it hasn't been difficult. Wanting children as we did. Sex without them, quite frankly, grows a little stale. I only wish she was stronger so that we might enjoy other activities.'

He paused before continuing. 'As regards intellect: plenty of men in our position in society would laugh you to scorn. They regard wives as breeding machines and when that's finished they're quite happy to take a mistress.'

Vince looked to where his wife and Kate were helping Jamie roll a snowball along the edge of the loch. Still very much in love, Vince found it incredible to envisage a day when he might wake up to find love turned sour and desire turned stale.

Conan watched his anxious expression and smiled consolingly. 'It does happen,' he said softly. 'But thankfully, not to us.'

Above their heads, the sky darkened, shadowed by heavy clouds.

It was suddenly cold. Intensely cold as the first snowflakes fell and their breath hung in icy globules upon the still air.

The storm, bringing events that were to change their lives for ever, was about to begin.

Chapter Two

To Faro, watching from the road, the scene was momentarily breathtaking. As the sky above the loch unloosed its burden, snowflakes floated down, thick and gentle as goosefeathers, on a scene from one of Jamie's favourite picture books. The skaters disappeared behind a translucent veil as the winter day died earlier than usual.

Vince's carriage was parked nearby in readiness to take them home. The coachman, Brent, sprang down and opened the door.

'I think I'll walk, thank you,' said Faro.

The man regarded him with astonishment. 'You'll get soaked, sir.'

But Faro pretended not to hear as he walked quickly back towards Newington. Above his head the massive expanse of Arthur's Seat, stretching high into the sky, resembled more than ever a lion couchant. Dwarfing humanity, it turned them into an army of tiny creatures minute as insects and of little consequence to an extinct volcano which had been comfortably ensconced millions of years before the dinosaurs walked the earth.

To his right lay Solomon's Tower. Sir Hedley Marsh, the eccentric aristocrat known as the 'Mad

Bart', had occupied its crumbling walls for countless years, long before the handsome houses that crept out beyond the city walls to take root in the ancient monastic fields on Edinburgh's southern boundaries became the suburbs of Newington and Priestfield.

Some old folk still hidebound by superstitions believed that the Mad Bart had the secret of immortality, a warlock as old as the tower whose early history had vanished into the mists of time.

Indeed, at first glance the stones and mortar of its construction blended so skilfully with the rocky backdrop of Arthur's Seat as to suggest that Solomon's Tower might have evolved from the landscape, spewed up ready-made from one of the ancient eruptions that had shaped the city of Edinburgh.

It was remote from any other building by mortal hands, and many were the tales of saints and devils, blessings and a fair amount of curses associated with its mysterious presence.

Legend told of an ancient tunnel leading from the cellars into a stone-vaulted room inside the hill where King Arthur sat with his knights at a round table, at his hand a silver horn, awaiting the clarion call which one day would summon him from sleep to ride out and save Britain. Needless to say no such passage had ever been found. If such had existed outside man's colourful imagination, then it had collapsed long ago.

More matter-of-fact history hinted at the tower as a refuge for the Knights Templar befriended by King Robert the Bruce after their flight from Jerusalem.

Then there were darker, more sinister tales of the Tower being used as a meeting place for conspirators, Mary Queen of Scots in particular. She was a lady always good for romance, and rumour had it that she frequently halted en route from Edinburgh to Craigmillar Castle for clandestine meetings with the dangerously attractive Lord Bothwell. Encounters which were the prelude to Lord Darnley's murder and the Stuart tragedy that changed the course of Scotland's history.

Such were Faro's thoughts that day, for the Tower looked more forbidding than usual behind a curtain of drifting snowflakes.

It seemed deserted and, according to Kate, her uncle, growing steadily frailer and more withdrawn, had retreated to one room. His innumerable and disreputable cats had also gone into steady decline since she and Conan had taken up residence.

Some had turned feral, lured away to join forces with the few wild cats who, according to hunters, still roamed the secret caves and environs of Arthur's Seat. Kate had firmly reduced the remaining numbers by the practical method of drowning unwanted litters who could not be fielded to cat-loving acquaintances among her husband's and Vince's patients.

This wise move had been followed by the introduction of a dog into the household: a splendid, large, warlike creature of bewildering and suspiciously wolflike ancestry whose presence had doubtless speeded up the general exodus of the more timid members of the feline tribe.

Nero (such was his name) was of pony-like proportions so enormous that he could have swallowed two of the kittens in one gulp, a thought that Faro, although no cat lover except for his housekeeper's beloved Rusty, cared little to dwell upon.

There was no doubt about it, Nero had by fair means or foul succeeded in reducing the cat population to five females of antique years and loyally undaunted spirits, still recognised by Sir Hedley and called fondly by name.

'They look as old as himself,' Conan had muttered to Faro on a visit. 'Probably live for ever too.'

Kate was amused. 'My husband doesn't like cats. He suspects them of having extra-sensory powers, streets ahead of us poor humans.'

Faro approved of the Pursleys. They were a good influence on the Mad Bart and there was no doubt in anyone's mind that he was both saner and cleaner, despite his failing health, since their advent. Well acquainted with the Tower's ruinous condition within and without, Faro was astonished at its transformation into a comfortable elegant home with curtained windows, carpeted stone floors and stairs. Brass and tarnished silver gleamed under Kate's care, and unspeakably foul upholstery had been replaced by pristine covers.

Uncle Hedley willingly provided funds for such alterations but turned his face resolutely against servants or housekeeper. Frail pretty Kate got her way by being allowed a daily maid to help out in the kitchen. 'That is all I need. I can do the rest.'

The snow was heavier now and Faro decided on the short cut home along Coffin Lane. Once site of the town gibbet, in kindlier times and weather it was a favourite haunt for lovers and a quick passage to the golf course.

Newington lay ahead with its prosperous newly built villas. Candles gleaming in the windows threw golden shadows on ghostly banks of hedges and garden walls. Trees glistened white and thrust out spectral arms, dripping diamonds of snow where the light touched them.

Uncurtained windows revealed shadowy glimpses of decorated trees while closer proximity brought sounds of children's laughter, indicative of parties afoot and still to come.

'Christmas is a-coming . . .'

Here it was indeed, waiting just around the corner. All the excitement, and adding to the yearly magic, a visit from his beloved daughter Rose now teaching in Glasgow. Faro sighed happily, a contented man as he let himself into his front door.

Leaving his snow-covered greatcoat and hat in the vestibule, he climbed the stairs to his study. He loved the smooth touch of the banisters beneath his hand and as always he sniffed the air. Mrs Brook's beeswax polish mingled with roasting meat and bread from her kitchen.

These were the smells of homecoming through the years; at the end of many a long and trying day reaching this dear familiar place, his haven of rest.

But he could not deny to himself that there was a wind of change blowing through Sheridan Place, a shadow of the future. He recognised with a pang of almost overwhelming sadness that in the years since Vince's marriage his own world had moved on. Every day he expected news that there would be another brother or a sister for Jamie and that his rooms would be desperately needed for nannies and maids.

They would be tactful, on no account willing to distress him, of course, with a feeling of urgency. Nevertheless he secretly wondered how much longer he could remain in this house and if any of the family suspected the direction his own thoughts were taking.

Once before, guiltily aware that his occupation of much-needed accommodation had made it necessary for Vince to take surgery premises in Minto Place, he had suggested moving out.

Cries of indignation had met his proposal. Vince and Olivia had warned him never, never to mention such a thing again.

'This is your home, Stepfather. Always was.'

'No question about it,' Olivia put in. 'We are the intruders. We must take a larger house.'

And that was that. Now there was a third partner in the ever-expanding practice in this thriving suburb. A newly graduated doctor had been introduced.

Full of his own importance, Angus Spens seemed very young and know-it-all to the senior doctors. He also happened to be the only son of Superintendent Spens, head of the Central Office of the Edinburgh City Police and Detective Inspector Faro's superior.

Superintendent Spens had succeeded Mackintosh, Faro's old sparring partner, who had retired, alas, without the knighthood he had hoped for.

As the most senior detective Faro had been offered promotion. Much to everyone's surprise but his own, he had refused. The idea of sitting behind a desk watching other detectives solve his crimes appalled him. After thirty years, he decided that if he moved on, it would not be up into the superintendent's office but away from Edinburgh altogether, a clean break to indulge his dreams of travel. In a word, retire. And if boredom overtook him there was, he told himself, always the possibility of private investigations.

Yes, travel was the answer, with his own bachelor establishment of two rooms in the heart of the city. An admirable idea.

He had scarcely had time to remove his boots when he heard Vince's carriage arrive back from the loch and the swift patter of Jamie's footsteps on the stairs.

'G'npa help Jamie – make snowman — '

After Jamie, trooped the grown-ups followed by Mrs Brook, carrying into the dining room a late afternoon tea of gargantuan proportions. Smiling indulgently, the housekeeper was also Jamie's willing slave.

'We won't wait for Dr Pursley, Mrs Brook,' said Vince, and to Faro, 'He's gone to the surgery to see if there are any urgent calls.' He shook his head. 'We're afraid this bitter weather might carry off some of our influenza victims. It looks like being an epidemic, unless we're very fortunate.'

'I thought Dr Spens was on duty this evening,' Kate sighed, rather peevishly, taking Jamie onto her knee.

Vince laughed. 'He is indeed. But young Angus isn't quite conscientious enough to please Conan. Once or twice he's failed to make visits. And that's the unforgivable sin in a surgery like ours.'

'Conan considers him quite inadequate. Too young and frivolous by far,' said Kate.

Vince smiled. 'Time will change that.' He looked

at her. 'Sometimes I think Conan cares more about the practice than I do.'

'Before Jamie came I couldn't keep you away,' said Olivia, with an adoring glance in his direction. 'A succession of sleepless nights cured all that, made you value your leisure.'

Kate, hugging Jamie close, kissing his soft curls, said wistfully: 'Children do change lives so much, don't they?'

Her sad voice struck a forlorn chord. In the silence that followed, Jamie swooping off her knee towards Faro with a jam-laden scone was a welcome diversion.

Holding the wee lad to his heart, Faro looked at the scene and wondered what had ever made him think of voluntarily leaving this beloved family.

He looked fondly at Vince, who had always been an integral part of his criminal investigations. His attitude to life was more conservative than his step-father's, and he bitterly resented changes, a conservatism intensified by his newly acquired social status as a middle-class Edinburgh doctor with an ever-increasing circle of influential friends and golf acquaintances.

When Vince's previous partner in the practice had decided to go to Canada the search for a replacement had been less tedious than Vince had imagined. The 37-year-old doctor from Glasgow, Dr Conan Pursley, had applied for the vacancy as his wife wished to take care of an elderly relative in Edinburgh.

Vince had never liked Sir Hedley and was disgusted by the sordid conditions of his establishment, but took consolation from the fact that Conan at least regarded staying there as a temporary measure.

Weary of Vince's incessant grumbles, Faro advised him sternly that if the Pursleys chose to live at Solomon's Tower out of a sense of responsibility to Kate's uncle, then he must accept that their domestic arrangements were none of his business and learn to tolerate occasional meetings with the old man with good grace.

Faro observed these meetings with suppressed amusement, aware that Sir Hedley, who had always doted on Vince and never neglected any opportunity of enlarging their acquaintance, had transferred his frustrated overtures of friendship to Vince's wife and child.

Now each time Olivia walked towards the loch where ducks and geese were to be fed by Jamie, Sir Hedley would race out from the tower, waving some toy or object that he was sure 'your wee lad' would like. Vince might scowl as much as he liked, but Olivia had a soft spot for the old man. She felt sorry for him living alone all those years and was glad he was to be taken care of at last.

In truth, she found his old-world charm and courtesy quite captivating and was prepared to listen for hours to his stories about the bad old Regency days before that young upstart Victoria came to the throne and made everyone painfully aware that they must maintain their respectability, or be shunned for lack of it.

Olivia felt that people who had lived then had a high old time of it one way and another. She was impressed that Sir Hedley's acquaintances at aristocratic shooting parties had included many notorious actresses, as well as members of the Royal Family, and he had some interesting and wicked scandals to relate.

Now helping himself to a second piece of cake, Faro listened idly to the conversation around the table.

Kate was having problems since Sir Hedley had met her maid in the area of the barred rooms on the upper floor.

'He was furious, sent her packing on the spot.'

'How awful,' said Olivia. 'What on earth does he keep there that is so precious?'

Kate shrugged. Not even Conan or herself were allowed across the threshold of what he called his 'old charter room'.

'An old man's junk room, according to Conan, full of mementoes of a misspent youth. A locked room, with the keys conveniently lost. I do confess that I feel it might be something more sinister he keeps up there.'

Faro remained silent. He decided not to enlighten them on his own knowledge of what that upper room of the Tower contained. Such knowledge might lead to overwhelming and ill-advised curiosity. Best let the past be.

Resisting further offers of tea, Kate groaned: 'I'll never eat supper after this.'

Olivia went to the window. 'Kate dear, you can't possibly walk back to the Tower. The snow's heavier than ever – look, the garden's covered completely since we came in.'

'Why don't you both stay the night here?' said

19

Vince. 'Brent can go round and collect Conan from the surgery.'

'A great idea,' said Olivia enthusiastically. 'I'll get Mrs Brook to make up a bed for you— '

But Kate was adamant. 'I must go. Nero has to be fed and Uncle Hedley will go to bed hungry unless I prepare supper for him. He's terribly absent-minded about mealtimes, you know.'

'Then take our carriage, if you must go. And take some of this food with you,' said Vince firmly.

'Do,' said Olivia. 'Mrs Brook will be delighted. She hates waste.'

Ten minutes later Kate was on her way home. Goodnights said, the carriage departed through the snow and Olivia carried a sleepy Jamie up to bed while Vince and Faro returned to the dining room where Mrs Brook had stoked up the fire.

Stretching out their legs to the blaze they shared a nightcap, a splendid single-malt whisky.

Faro sighed contentedly. This was his favourite time of the day.

It was a great life. A great life, here with his beloved family. Who could ask for more?

Who indeed?

He was to remember those happy hours that evening with the snow falling gently in the garden beyond the windows.

It would be a long time before such content was to be his again.

Chapter Three

They found the first victim lying beneath the blood-soaked snow in Coffin Lane.

PC Dean, heading towards Dalkeith Road on his normal beat, had taken the short cut and made the discovery by the merest chance of observing a hump of newly fallen snow with an effusion of pink.

His immediate idea was that some wounded animal lay beneath. Closer inspection revealed a white hand, a cold, dead, unmoving woman's hand. She had been thrust into the snow-filled ditch during the night and the heavy fall of snow had hidden the terrible sight until morning.

PC Dean knew what he was about. A practical, well-trained policeman not given to bouts of panic, he knelt down and, carefully scraping the snow away, followed that dead hand up to arm, shoulder and then to neck, although there was little possibility of the woman still being alive.

At last the dead face was revealed, a ghastly grey with the snow melting on eyes that were wide open and frozen in death.

She had been stabbed through the chest.

He looked desperately around the still-empty landscape. The procedure to be followed was particular.

Find a doctor in case there was hope of resuscitation and then summon his superior officer. In this case he was fortunate in having both nearby.

It was unlikely that anyone would disturb the corpse or be in the vicinity in such weather but PC Dean lost no more time. Leaving the scene he plunged towards Sheridan Place. He moved as quickly as was humanly possible through several inches of snow, marking as he did so that, apart from a few animal tracks, the whole of Edinburgh seemed to have been brought to a complete standstill.

He had the world and the corpse he had just left to himself, and trying not to keep looking back over his shoulder as if the old man with the scythe might be following, he was greatly relieved to find Inspector Faro and Dr Laurie at their breakfast.

Dr Conan Pursley was with them, having been benighted and unable to return to Solomon's Tower after attending the deathbed of a sick patient in the influenza outbreak.

Within minutes all three were hastening back to Coffin Lane with Dean, a passing errand-boy entrusted with a shilling in his pocket to alert the Central Office that the mortuary carriage would be required.

Faro knelt to examine the woman's body, wondering why murders at Christmastime seemed so much more gross, their brutality a further blasphemy against the season of goodwill. As PC Dean explained the circumstances of his gruesome find, he knew that the heavy snowfall also helped to establish the time of death as sometime during the hours of the previous night. It also destroyed any hope of finding clues.

PC Dean stood by watching them carefully scrape the snow off the body. Meanwhile the small crowd who wait in readiness to gravitate towards any disaster were gathering and had to be kept at bay.

Faro shuddered for as the body was uncovered a great effusion of blood spread across the snow. The stab wound in the woman's chest re-opened allowing the blood to run freely again.

The three men stepped back sharply and Faro remembered in horror the old adage about victims bleeding when faced with their murderer.

He glanced quickly over his shoulder. Was one of the faces in the group of onlookers staring so curiously at the horrific tableau that of the killer returned to the scene of his crime?

Vince and Conan rose from their knees and he wondered if the same thought was in their minds as the woman's open eyes stared beyond them, beyond the confines of Coffin Lane towards the heights of Arthur's Seat.

Even so, the gaze of the three men followed in the same direction and rested on the only habitation, Solomon's Tower, which would have been encompassed in that wild-eyed, horrified last look at the world.

In ancient times this area had known many such grisly occurrences, thought Faro grimly: men slain in battles over the centuries, criminals hanged whose last earthly sight had been thus.

The silence was broken by the clanging bell of the police carriage; swerving dangerously, it finally came to rest some fifty yards away. There were sounds of protesting wheels and horses, men's shrill curses and at last two policemen struggled through the snow carrying a stretcher.

Young Dr Spens followed at their heels. 'Am I too late then?' His eagerness and barely concealed excitement as he stared down at the dead woman seemed all out of context with his young rosy face.

Conan muttered, 'Obvious, isn't it?'

'Been dead long, has she?' asked Angus cheerfully.

'Some time,' said Conan.

'Oh really?'

'Yes. If you were hoping for a chance to practise survival methods you are several hours too late,' was Conan's sarcastic reply.

Angus ignored him, pushing Vince aside. 'One moment please. May I?'

Kneeling down he carefully scrutinised the body on the stretcher as if he saw a murder victim every day. He pursed his lips at the stab wound and nodded authoritatively while over his shoulder Vince and Conan shook their heads.

As the policemen prepared to carry the corpse to the waiting mortuary carriage, Faro stretched forth his hand and carefully removed the woman's reticule, which was twisted round her wrist.

'I was about to do that myself, Inspector,' said Angus indignantly, a spoilt child deprived of a trophy. 'It may contain evidence, you know.'

'Indeed? Her murderer's name and address, perhaps?'

Angus coloured. 'No, her own, of course.'

Faro nodded. 'All right, lads, you may proceed.'

The small crowd let out a sigh as the body was bundled out of their sight as swiftly and in as dignified a manner as rigor would permit in the circumstances.

'You may accompany them if you so wish, Dr Spens,' said Faro, anxious to be rid of him.

'May I really, Inspector?' Angus replied with almost indecent eagerness to visit the mortuary.

Turning, he smiled sarcastically at Faro: 'Knowing your reputation, sir, no doubt you will have solved the case or at the very least produced a promising list of suspects by the time I get to the Central Office.'

Faro merely nodded. He had reached a few conclusions about the woman's identity, merely from observation. The soaked, shabby, dark dress and thin cloak indicated a servant girl, most probably from this area. Death had not been kind; she could have been anywhere between eighteen and forty.

The onlookers lingered and then dispersed unwillingly, trudging away back whence they had come, their drama over for the day. There was nothing more to see, but it gave them plenty to talk about for some time.

Vince and Conan remained with PC Dean in attendance, carefully scraping the snow from where the corpse had lain, but apart from the blood-stained ground there was a complete absence of any clues as to why the unfortunate woman had been murdered.

'Any sign of the murder weapon?' asked Vince.

'It could be anywhere in the vicinity,' said Faro. 'But we'll have to wait until the snow clears to be absolutely sure.'

They were aware that it could lie hidden for weeks before the thaw set in and indeed the heavy grey sky suggested there might be considerably more snow to fall, further hampering investigations.

Vince frowned. 'A broad-bladed knife was used and with considerable force, I should think.'

'Possibly a knife of the domestic kind. Kitchen, most likely. *Crime passionel*, perhaps. Looked like a servant,' said Conan, pointing to the reticule Faro was opening which the woman had not relinquished in the attack.

'It wasn't theft, that we can eliminate,' said Vince.

Faro nodded. 'Which leaves us with the first question of why, if this wasn't a random attack merely for theft, and rape seems unlikely.' They would not know for sure but there had been no disturbance or dishevelment of the woman's clothing.

'A jealous swain, tormented and angry,' suggested Conan.

Faro shrugged. The woman's body and the lack of evidence of a struggle had not suggested an attack where the victim had exchanged angry words with her assailant but rather that she was taken by surprise.

He opened the reticule, praying silently that it held some means of identification so that the search for her killer would not be impeded.

'Ah,' he said triumphantly. Their guess that she was a servant girl was correct. He took out a letter, wet but still legible, a former employer's reference recommending Molly Blaith for her excellent qualities of honesty and industry. It was headed 'To whom it may concern', and such letters were always the most guarded possession of anyone in domestic service.

'And there's more. Here!' He produced another

letter with a stamp on it addressed to a solicitor's firm in Queen Street. Opening it gingerly, he said: 'This is all we need. The poor girl had been sent out to post this by her employer, a Miss Errington in Minto Street.'

'Then we have something to go on,' sighed Vince.

Faro frowned. 'We do indeed. But why should she have chosen to walk down Coffin Lane right past a postbox at the end of her road?'

'The answer isn't too difficult. No doubt she had an assignation,' said Vince.

'Of course,' said Conan, 'with the murderer. A crime of passion, I'm surer of it every moment. He stabs her, rushes off in a panic. Let's face it, if he had had time to think it out, then he wouldn't have left anything to reveal her identity.'

Faro considered this possibility thoughtfully, staring at the sodden patch of snow-cleared ground where she had lain.

'Perhaps and perhaps not,' said Vince. 'She might have met him earlier, he attacked her and she ran away from him – ran down here.'

Faro put an end to speculations which merely confused the issue. 'I expect much will be revealed by a visit to Miss Amelia Errington.'

He was dreading the encounter, expecting tears, vapours, fainting and the application of smelling salts.

He felt his worst fears were to be confirmed when he encountered Dr Mills leaving the house.

They had a slight acquaintance through Vince's

practice and Dr Mills looked at him curiously after an affable greeting.

'You are Miss Errington's physician?' said Faro.

'Indeed, yes.'

'Is she ill?'

Dr Mills smiled. 'Not exactly ill, but in poor health generally. She has a heart condition – why do you ask?'

'Because your attendance may be needed, sir. Her maid's body has just been found in Coffin Lane.'

'Good Lord. Not Molly?'

'Alas, yes.'

Dr Mills gripped his bag firmly. 'Then I must go to her. An accident, I take it?'

'She's dead, I'm afraid. Her body has been removed to the police mortuary.'

The doctor stared at him in disbelief and repeated, 'The police?'

'We have reason to believe she was murdered.'

'Good Lord,' repeated Mills. 'This is dreadful – dreadful. Then I had better come with you. This is very bad news for Miss Errington.'

'They were close?'

'Indeed yes. Molly was more than a personal maid. She was also a companion.'

Faro decided to take advantage of this fortuitous meeting with the doctor who probably knew more than most the workings of Miss Errington's household.

He put a delaying hand on Mills' arm as they climbed the steps. 'Tell me, sir, can you think of any reason why Molly should have been murdered?'

The doctor frowned. 'None at all.'

'Was she a patient of yours? Doctors frequently have intimate information unknown to even the closest friends or relatives.'

Mills smiled. 'I see what you are getting at, sir. The secrets of the confessional.' He shook his head. 'Alas, I'm afraid I have to disappoint you. Molly never consulted me on any occasion and as far as I know she is – was – a strong and healthy young woman.'

'Would you have considered her the kind of young woman who might have enemies?'

Mills stared at him for a moment. Then he laughed. 'I see what you are driving at, Inspector. You are hinting that she might have had a jealous or over-zealous young man.'

'I must confess I was hoping for something of the sort, sir.'

Mills shook his head. 'Then I am sorry to have to disappoint you once again. Molly was completely devoted to her mistress and as far as I have gathered she had no other life outside this house.'

Regarding Faro's doubtful expression, he laughed softly. 'You will understand a lot more when you meet Miss Errington.'

Chapter Four

Admitted after several onslaughts on the doorbell by a scared-looking maid obviously relieved to see that one of the two gentlemen on the doorstep was Dr Mills, they were shown into the sitting room while she went to see if her mistress was receiving callers.

Suspecting that they might be in for a long wait, Faro used this admirable opportunity to invite the doctor to fill in some details of Miss Errington's background.

'Her father served Her Majesty in India. Her mother died when she was fourteen and she devoted her entire life to taking care of her father. Molly has been with her for the past two, or is it three years . . .'

Faro found himself listening to a familiar tale of an only child, a daughter who gave up a life of her own to look after a bereaved parent, only to find when death released her from her duties that the marriageable years had also vanished.

More fortunate than some who were doomed to single blessedness, Amelia Errington could at least enjoy the remainder of her years in comfort, if not the happiness that wealth could not buy.

The house, a typical middle-class Georgian villa, was already showing signs of luxury somewhat decayed. There was an Aubusson carpet, elegant furniture and bric-a-brac on small tables. The stern and forbidding expressions of the family portraits on the walls indicated states of mind not noticeably cheered in the graduation to family photographs on the grand piano.

The atmosphere, those first impressions, told Faro much about the house's owner and were confirmed when Miss Errington entered the room in her wheelchair.

Faro was introduced but left the doctor to break the horrific news. The invalid Miss Errington was shocked. However, she did not faint or have a heart attack, armoured from her earliest years against showing any emotions relating to the fate of that lesser breed of mortals, the servants.

Her attitude showed clearly that it was the stigma attached to such a dreadful happening that affected her most. What interpretation would her influential friends and acquaintances, to say nothing of neighbours, put upon such a happening?

Molly was after all only a servant, but Miss Errington's house had given her shelter and she had paid her wages. Murder taints those nearest regardless of their innocence and might well be calculated to throw considerable doubts on matters relating to her mistress's reliability and respectability.

'How will you manage without her?' asked Dr Mills gently.

Miss Errington turned to him from a somewhat glazed contemplation of the garden beyond the window. 'I have a housemaid, Adie; she answered the door. I presume she is competent to deal with such elementary matters until I find a replacement.'

And quite unexpectedly there were tears. She sobbed for a few moments, swiftly applying a lace handkerchief.

Dr Mills patted her shoulder, and Faro cleared his throat, embarrassed into thinking that he had been too hasty in his judgement of her character. Her reaction had merely been shock and disbelief. She had a soft heart after all.

She looked up at the men appealingly. 'I really don't know what I'll do without Molly. She was absolutely devoted to me.'

'Has she any family?' Faro asked.

Miss Errington shook her head. 'None. She was a workhouse child. I took her on trust and she repaid it well. She was eighteen when I took her in. She had been a servant with a very respectable family who were moving to Spain. Although her working life began with scrubbing floors in a local hospital, I was prepared to overlook this since she took enormous pride in having risen in the world from such lowly beginnings.'

She sighed. 'A very reliable girl, she had excellent references, of course,' she added, a fact which Faro already knew.

'A young woman, surely she had some private life, friends in the area perhaps?' asked Faro.

Miss Errington looked suspicious and a trifle apprehensive at the word 'friends'. 'Your meaning, Inspector?' she said stiffly.

'I mean, madam, perhaps a young man.'

Miss Errington, who had never experienced feel-

ings of being in love and therefore hadn't the least
idea what he was talking about, was outraged at such
a wicked idea.

'Of course she didn't have a – young man.' She
spat out the words, managing to make them sound
an obscenity. 'I assure you she was entirely devoted
to me.'

Faro smiled. 'Quite so, quite so.' Apparently Miss
Errington moved in a wilderness where the natural
inclinations of man and womankind did not exist. A
wilderness devoid of the emotion that kept the world
turning and carried those who fell beneath its spell
beyond the call of duty to their employers.

'Is there anything else, Inspector?'

'I should like to see her room.'

Miss Errington was not at all pleased at this
request and for a moment he thought she was going
to refuse. Such behaviour in someone less invalidish
would have made him immediately suspicious.

Adie was summoned and waited at the bedroom
door, eyeing him apprehensively as he opened the
rickety cupboard and looked through the two drawers
in the shabby chipped chest to reveal darned underwear and stockings. A nightgown lay neatly folded
beside what was probably poor Molly's only other
dress.

'Done something wrong, has she?' demanded Adie
as he closed the door.

'Not that I know about,' said Faro. 'Was she a friend
of yours?' he added hopefully of the shivering kitchen
maid. As she watched him she rubbed together hands
blue with cold. Her nose was red and the house icy
except for the fire in Miss Errington's sitting room.

The thin dress under the starched white apron and cap looked hopelessly inadequate to keep Adie warm although he doubted that such a thought had ever crossed Miss Errington's mind, cosily wrapped in cashmere shawls against the chilly corridors.

'That one!' Faro realised that Adie was speaking not of present injustices by her employer, but launching a tirade against Molly.

'A friend, that one! Not likely! Proper snob she was, thought herself somebody, being the mistress's companion. Tried to imitate her proper manners. It was "do this, Adie, do that", never a kind word. Above her station, she copied the mistress, even the way she talked,' she added darkly.

'Did she have friends outside the house?' Faro asked and Adie's lips twitched into a sneer.

'Not her. Never went out nowhere except with the mistress. Close as two peas in a pod, they were, probably had hopes of being left something in her will when she goes.'

Faro went to the door.

'Is that it then? Seen enough, have you?'

'I would like to see your kitchen, if I may.'

Adie looked at him. 'What on earth for?'

He pretended not to hear the question and with a shrug she led the way down the back stairs into a kitchen which nursed an inadequate fire and was only marginally less cold and forbidding than the rest of the house.

She was surprised at his request to inspect the cutlery drawer.

'The best silver's kept in the dining room. Locked away. Is some of it missing too? Is that what's up?

Done a bunk with the silver, has she?' she asked eagerly.

'Not as far as I know.' Opening the drawer on a formidable array of unhappy-looking knives, forks and spoons which had seen better years, he said, 'What about carving knives?'

She stared at him, frowned and said: 'We have only the one, and it's hanging on the nail – over there – by the stove.'

He nodded. 'Any other long sharp knives?'

'No. Just the one. Why do you ask that?'

Ignoring the question he hurried towards the door leading upstairs and into the hall. 'Are you and Molly the only staff Miss Errington employs?'

'Yes. She doesn't hold with armies of servants. Waste of money— '

'Thank you, Adie. You've been very helpful.'

Emerging from the baize door, he observed Miss Errington in the sitting room with Dr Mills attentively pushing her wheelchair towards him.

'Well, Inspector, what did you find?' Miss Errington demanded. There was a hint of sarcasm in her voice, as if she knew the answer that there was nothing of a personal nature in the bleak, cold room to indicate that Molly knew the identity of her murderer.

'Nothing of value. But thank you for your assistance, madam.' And preparing to leave as Dr Mills offered consoling words to his patient, Faro produced the contents of Molly's reticule. 'There was an unposted letter to your solicitor, madam.'

'How very tiresome. It was most urgent.' She tut-tutted. 'Wretched girl.' And suddenly realising how the wretched girl had met her end, she said stiffly, 'Thank you for letting me know. Perhaps you would be so good as to put it in the mailbox at the end of the street.'

Faro bowed assent, waiting politely on the doorstep to be joined by Dr Mills. He stared up at the windows. 'Big house for one invalid lady to keep up.'

Dr Mills smiled. 'Miss Errington belongs to the old school. Values her privacy above all else. Has plenty of money, you would guess, but refuses to countenance the upkeep of a flock of servants in accordance with her station in life.'

Such ideals obviously did not run to a sturdy fire or two, and Faro shivered as he trudged through the snow down the Pleasance towards the High Street.

There would be a good fire in his office and a good strong cup of tea at his command.

Hoping there would be something more in the nature of evidence relating to Molly's murder, Faro was eager to see the police surgeon's report which stated that the stab wound was superficial, not severe enough to be fatal, having missed any vital organ. She had bled to death in the snow.

Faro sighed. This frenzied but inept murder attempt confirmed his own conclusions. Namely that Molly had some secret life beyond the walls of the house he had just left, but spared her employer's feelings, or more likely spared herself the chill wind of Miss Errington's displeasure.

Had he been a betting man, he would have put

his money on Conan's theory of a jealous lover who had lured her to her death in Coffin Lane, almost certain to be empty on such a night.

Why, was the first question. Who, would come later. A married man, perhaps, and, desperate to escape from Miss Errington's clutches, was Molly threatening to reveal all to his wife?

Blackmail was a common enough occurrence, a costly business, which all too often rebounded and cost the blackmailer his or her life.

Whatever the reason, their meeting had been urgent enough to occupy all Molly's thoughts and let her walk past the post-box carrying her mistress's important letter, her excuse for leaving the house in such appalling weather.

Her agitation and forgetfulness had been greater than her regard for that lady's wrath, which Faro suspected might be considerable.

Murderers, he knew from thirty years' experience, were usually known to their victims and most likely to be found in the family circle or in the ranks of close friends.

In Molly's case, for family circle, he read Miss Errington or some other occupant of the house. An unlikely enough choice between an invalid and a shivering kitchen maid. Although Adie disliked the upstart Molly he could not see either maid or mistress blindly hitting out with the murder weapon, that still-missing knife which was not from Miss Errington's kitchen.

He was almost certain that knowing the victim's identity, it would not take long for evidence to mount up that would point clearly in the murderer's direction.

But events were already taking shape which were to change his mind and make nonsense of his careful theories.

Chapter Five

Faro had just set foot in the Central Office when Superintendent Spens appeared at his door.

'Another murder, have you, Faro?' he asked. His somewhat weary tone indicated that such events happened every day and that his chief inspector attracted them as other men attracted the present influenza epidemic.

Superintendent Spens ('No relative to Sir Patrick of that ilk' he insisted) had replaced Superintendent Mackintosh, recently retired, his decent pension failing to compensate for the list of woes with which he regaled listeners on the subject of 'How I failed to qualify for my knighthood'.

Despite the abrasive quality of their relationship over the years, Faro missed him. His successor was of a different breed from Mackintosh, who had worked his way up from the ranks, a fact that he had been proud to remember and keen not to let anyone else ever forget. It was perhaps the only ground for agreement between Faro and himself.

Percival Spens was college-educated, he had left the University of St Andrews with first class honours in history. Many of the rank and file in the Central Office suspected that his appointment came by virtue of influence rather than a lifetime's devotion to crime, if such an unhappy and grisly occupation could qualify for the description 'devotion'.

Superintendent Spens was as keen as his predecessor had been that no one should forget his impressive background. Addicted to Latin tags, which mostly fell on deaf ears and produced dazed expressions among his subordinates, he resorted to quoting Shakespeare and was somewhat dismayed that Chief Inspector Faro, who had scant education, was an authority on the Bard. Faro even had the temerity to correct his superior officer ever so politely: 'That was from *Othello* not *Hamlet*, sir;' and 'May I point out, sir, that is from *Henry IV Part 2*, not *Henry V.*'

His ego thus dashed, the superintendent took refuge in the more obscure works, hoping to catch Faro at a disadvantage.

He was unsuccessful. Those who knew the inspector hid their smiles, aware that his retentive memory was remarkable; he was able to remember not only the words but the page they appeared on. And Shakespeare, Sir Walter Scott and Charles Dickens were foremost in Faro's leisure reading.

'Who ever heard of a policeman spouting Shakespeare?' asked Mrs Spens, who was born of the same mould as her husband and had been carefully chosen for her breeding. 'Sounds to me as if he hasn't half enough to keep him occupied, Percival,' she added severely, sharing with her husband the opinion that education should be restricted to the upper classes. 'It is my belief that no servant should be allowed anything stronger than the Bible and that only in an expurgated form. In the wrong hands the teachings of Christ might well be subject to misinterpretation,' she whispered with a shudder. 'You know the sort of sentiment, Percival, about the meek inheriting the earth.'

Spens patted her hand sympathetically. 'Quite right, m'dear, can't have the servants getting ideas above their station in life. What would become of us all then? I agree, my dear, some carefully chosen passages and that strictly reserved for a couple of hours on a Sunday.'

'Ah, blood will out, there's no doubt about it,' he was fond of quoting at the golf club to anyone prepared to listen, and sadly there were quite a few who agreed with his philosophy. Spens was regarded, however, as something of a bore, to be avoided if possible, especially as this was his hobby horse to be ridden on every occasion, an excuse for being an indifferent golfer.

'You can always tell. Look at those two young doctors,' he once said to his partner, patiently waiting to play his next shot. 'A fine example of breeding. High foreheads, classical features, splendid bone structure. No one could mistake them for the criminal classes.'

The doctors in question playing the hole ahead and unaware that they were the subject of Spens' attention were, in fact, Vince and Conan.

When it was pointed out to him that Dr Laurie was in fact Inspector Faro's stepson, Spens shuddered delicately but was prepared to overlook this shortcoming as a gross mismanagement of fate. He took refuge in mutterings about the Orkney people being different and that one could not account for the Viking influence, thereby completely missing the point that there was no blood relationship between the two men.

Conan Pursley did a wicked impersonation of the superintendent. He found him vastly amusing, until the day he was partnered with Spens in a match and was earnestly and enthusiastically discussing his work with the mentally disturbed. Spens sniffed and said abruptly that he was wasting his time and his medical knowledge in such endeavours and that all such people should be exterminated.

'Painlessly as possible, of course,' he added hastily, seeing Conan's grim expression. 'No one wants to cause them any extra suffering.'

Needless to say when reports of such encounters reached Faro's ears, he was not amused either. Those who saw them together guessed there was no love lost. If ever two men stepped off on the wrong foot, the superintendent and his senior detective were the perfect examples.

Right from the first meeting, Spens had been resentful, believing that Faro should have done the decent thing and retired at the same time as Mackintosh, instead of hanging on and keeping the exalted position from some younger man.

'After all, you'll soon be fifty. Can't expect expert efficiency at criminal-catching at that age. Stands to reason, body slows down. All that wear and tear through the years.'

Faro was outraged and kept his temper with some difficulty. It was clear that Spens based criminal detection on physical fitness rather than, first and most important, a fit and active mind.

What angered him more was that he was only a few years senior to Spens, but whereas that was perfectly all right for a superintendent sitting behind a desk, it was not the thing for a policeman regarded as finished at fifty despite all evidence to the contrary.

Or was it? He had to admit that on bad days his body was beginning to show ominous signs of wear, the effects of long-term ill usage, an unhealthy style of living with food too often forgotten or replaced by liquid meals in the form of drams or pints of ale. Thirty years of grappling with criminals had resulted in bullet wounds, knife scars and now a regrettable tendency for broken bones and wounds not to heal as fast these days.

Once he could ignore minor afflictions, now he was forced to admit that he no longer had sole command of that excellent working machine, his body. Of late the frosts of winter seemed to seek out all those injuries which were his legacy for active service with the Edinburgh City Police. Honourable scars, proudly won, but distinctly tiresome to a man whose round of criminal-catching might involve walking fifteen miles a day regardless of weather.

He was blessed with an iron constitution and a bone structure twice as strong as most mortal men, and this accounted for his survival against fearful odds. The gift of his Viking ancestry had seen him through many potential disasters. That and an extra sense, the 'second sight' his mother called it, warned him of dangers existing and gave him premonitions of those to come, hovering unshakeable and invisible, clouding his waking hours.

He fully realised that if the machine was no longer in good working order then he must think sensibly in terms of retirement, let younger men take over. Perhaps nature was telling him why he felt so apprehensive of what the future had in store. Or was it merely seasonal? he thought hopefully. The effect of gloomy winter days and chilly risings at six o'clock, whereas on summer mornings he cheerfully greeted the birdsong in his garden at first light.

Persuading himself that the weather was to blame, since the thought of an inactive life horrified him more than a quick sharp death, he was already dreading the approach of the next decade of his life.

He could not stay young for ever; growing old was inevitable, as natural as birth itself. Sometimes he was aware that at the back of his mind was a plan to defeat that dreadful prospect of retirement. He would use all the experience and expertise of his days with Edinburgh City Police and set up as a private detective, able to pick and choose what cases most intrigued him.

Travel had always been his other love; now he would have a chance to move further afield with his investigations as well as being free to go to Orkney and see his daughter Emily and her new husband on a long visit.

And then there was America and his ex-Sergeant Detective, Danny McQuinn. A new continent, new people and ways of life; that was the thought that most pleased and exhilarated him, for he had never been out of Britain in his life, hardly ever travelling any further south than the borders.

What a world of excitement awaited him beyond the confines of the English Channel. Paris, Italy, the Black Forest – he could visit them all and if he was bored he could confidently offer his services to the local chiefs of police!

Spens was regarding him across the desk. 'Got any evidence this time?'

'Not yet, sir.' He began patiently to explain the manner of the discovery.

Spens waved it aside. 'I know all that. Angus came in with a report on his way to the mortuary.' Head on one side, he beamed. 'My lad did very well, I gather. Very helpful to your two doctors. They must be quite proud of him.'

Pausing to give Faro a chance of favourable comment and disappointed not to receive any, he continued, 'Need a strong stomach for his kind of work. Always wanted to work on crime cases. Fascinated by all my books on the subject. Had to keep some of them out of his way, I can tell you, when he was a wee lad. His mother thought such things weren't decent reading for a youngster.'

He sighed happily. 'A little more experience and he'll be ready to assist the police surgeon. That should get it out of his system. He'll go far, I'm sure.' Again he paused. 'And what do you think, Faro?'

'Oh indeed, he'll go far, sir.' But Faro was careful not to state in which particular direction the overly ambitious young doctor would travel.

Later he sat down at his desk and wrote his report on the day's events, clearly and precisely, from the moment he had been summoned to the discovery of the body until it had left his sight to be carried to the police mortuary.

At this stage of the investigation, speculations were superfluous and he preferred to keep his observations to himself for the moment.

He glanced through some papers that needed his attention, put a note in his diary and hurried across to the Sheriff Court where he appeared briefly as a witness in a Customs and Excise fraud case.

The proceedings were lengthy and extremely tedious and he emerged feeling weary and dispirited. He had sat through so many identical cases that he almost welcomed a crime where he could use his own powers of deduction.

As he walked home down the Pleasance towards Newington, the church clock chimed four, but it was already dark, the road ahead filled with fitful moonlight.

A full moon, bright, exotic and mysterious, crept over Arthur's Seat. For some reason it made him think of Conan's story that nurses and wardens at the asylum walked warily when the moon was full.

'Throughout man's history, it has always been a time of vulnerability for the mentally disturbed. Even the mildest of patients become moody, their unpredictable behaviour dangerous to others as well as themselves.' Conan had smiled grimly. 'We were warned to look over our shoulders, constantly on guard for an outbreak of violence. Moonstruck madness, they call it.'

Chapter Six

There were voices in the hall as Faro opened his front door. Kate had been visiting Olivia and, about to leave, she was fastening her cloak with its silver brooch which she wore constantly. Among many more valuable jewels, Faro guessed this was her favourite.

When he had first admired the unusual design of an owl perched on a crescent moon alongside a smaller moon bisected by a cross, she had touched it fondly: 'The owl moons clasper. Family heirloom, you know. Very precious. Given to us by Prince Charles Edward Stuart while he was in the Highlands raising the clans.'

Faro had suppressed a smile. So many houses allegedly told the same romantic tale of a prince in the heather, that he had slept in as many beds as his thrice great-grandmother Queen Mary, a far greater number than would have been needed during his short time in Scotland.

Olivia and Vince had been suitably impressed but Faro had thought little of the brooch as a genuine antique or as a work of art until Conan's parents visited Solomon's Tower that autumn.

William Pursley, landscape gardener to the aristocracy, could not forgo giving advice on the dense undergrowth that passed as a garden. Such a neglected wilderness was an unforgivable sin that outraged his sensibilities and before they could protest he was out with a spade, digging vigorously at the stubborn, tangled weeds of centuries past.

Suddenly he called to them and they trooped out to be confronted by a large square stone, weathered by the passing centuries.

'It must have been here for hundreds of years, there's some sort of inscription under the lichen,' he said triumphantly. Taking a knife, while they watched intrigued, he carefully scraped away the thick green encrustations to reveal a large but exact replica of Kate's brooch.

'The owl moons clasper!' gasped Kate.

'The very same, dear. What a strange coincidence,' said her mother-in-law.

Sir Hedley, called upon to express an opinion, merely grunted. 'Never seen it before,' he said shortly and went back indoors, showing a complete lack of interest in their activities.

Kate, however, was very excited by the stone's discovery, certain that it must be connected with the missing French gold sent to Scotland in 1745 to finance the Young Pretender's disastrous uprising.

As they crowded round the stone, one glance told Faro that it was much older than Kate's clasper. Even lacking an archaeologist's knowledge, he realised that the stone must have formed part of the Templars' Chapel which had preceded the present Tower, and had probably played some significant role in their mystic rituals.

Faro's observations did not please Kate. She gave

him an angry glance, refusing to relinquish the romantic legend. Taking command of the situation she insisted that they dig a pit beneath the stone in search of the buried treasure.

'Think of it, what a find,' she said, clasping her hands and watching Conan and Vince hurling out spadesful of soil, ably directed and assisted by William Pursley and less enthusiastically by Faro.

Every time they stopped digging for lack of breath, or to ease aching backs, she leaned over excitedly, saying, 'Well, have you found something?' She was rewarded with a negative shake of the head, a groan and a sigh as more soil was flung out of the hole.

Watching them throw down their spades as darkness fell, Conan attempted to ameliorate his wife's disappointment at the broken dream of buried treasure with a promise to write to the Society of Antiquaries.

'I'll send them a drawing of the stone and the clasper. See if they know anything about its history.'

Faro sighed. This was not the first time he had encountered Charles Edward Stuart's missing French gold.

It had figured in an earlier case at Priorsfield when a skeleton, dug up in the gardens with a knife in its ribs, was assumed to be the missing Frenchman who had failed to reach his destination, the gold accounting for the sudden wealth of the owners of the then humble inn.

Faro had little faith in buried treasure. Mostly it turned out to be buried secrets best left unearthed, as he and Vince had found, more likely to destroy than enrich the inheritors.

Olivia was intrigued by Sir Hedley's lack of interest in such an exciting discovery.

'Why do they call him the Mad Bart?' she asked on the way home.

'It's just a local nickname,' said Vince.

'He seems harmless enough.' She sounded relieved. 'I mean, was he ever dangerous?'

Faro laughed. 'Not a bit. I understand he earned it from shouting abuse at passers-by, particularly royal carriages travelling along the road in front of the Tower, on what he regards as his property, en route from Holyrood Palace to Duddingston and beyond.'

'Maybe he's softened with age,' said Vince, 'but we have it on good authority that he used to rush out and shake his fist at them, shouting, "Hanoverian upstarts", "Go back to Germany", "German lairdies, the lot of you", and similar insults.'

Olivia giggled. 'How awful.'

'Particularly if you happened to be one of the outriders of Her Majesty's carriage,' said Faro. 'I will say for the Queen that she remains implacable, staring grimly in front, hopefully either too involved in admiring the scenery or stone deaf— '

'Or both!' said Vince.

' "Long live King Jamie, long live the Stuarts" were Sir Hedley's milder statements – it might be called disturbing the peace with treasonable conduct,' said Faro.

Solomon's Tower was and always had been a staunchly Jacobite stronghold from the days when Charles Edward Stuart visited it on his arrival in Edinburgh, dining with the then occupier and considering what to do next while his followers were somewhat more damply and inconveniently encamped outside.

The contemporary account read:

> The detachment passed without being observed by the garrison of Edinburgh Castle, so near as to hear them distinctly call their rounds, and arrived at the nether bow Port without meeting anybody on their way, and found the Flodden Wall of the Town which flanks the Pleasants [sic] and St Mary's Wynd mounted with cannon but no person arrived.
>
> Their demand for admission refused, Mr Murray [of Broughton] proposed to retire to a place called St Leonards hills [Arthur's Seat] and after securing themselves from the cannon of the Castle, to wait for orders from the Chevalier where to attack the town.

'It must have been a memorable occasion for the Prince staying in the Tower, if you are right about it having once been a Templars' Hospice,' said Olivia.

Faro nodded. 'As a building with a long and bad reputation, and the Prince known to be susceptible to omens, he must have been aware that this roof had often sheltered his thrice great-grandmother Queen Mary, and was her secret rendezvous with the Earl of Bothwell.'

'Indeed,' said Vince. 'They had both enjoyed its hospitality, and little good it had done either of them.'

'Or Scotland,' added Faro sadly. 'And Kate's brooch doesn't look like an ancient plaid pin to me.'

'It's just a replica,' said Olivia. 'She told me that the original was far too valuable historically and that it's kept in in a glass case in Edinburgh Castle alongside a modest amount of jewellery and miniatures belonging to Queen Mary, including the rosary she wore going to her execution. Such sad relics,' she added.

Now as Kate stood on the front doorstep at Sheridan Place, she sighed. 'What a glorious moon. So beautiful.' She touched her brooch. 'The clasper likes moonlight, the silver glows even brighter somehow.'

Across her shoulder, Olivia grinned at Faro. Too practical to take such nonsense seriously, and knowing Kate's romantic story, she was much readier to accept Faro's theory.

'Allow me to escort you to the surgery,' he said.

She laughed. 'Thank you, you're very kind, but Conan's visiting his parents today. He's worried about his mother.'

A shadow touched her face as she realised the reason for Faro's offer. A woman had been murdered not a quarter of a mile from where they stood.

'Brent is always available for Kate and Conan,' Olivia reminded Faro gently. 'Ah, there he is now.'

They watched the carriage disappear around the corner. A wisp of a final wave from Kate then Olivia said, 'The snow does look quite magical. Moonlight changes everything, doesn't it?'

Gazing up at the sky, Faro sighed. It was a time of such beauty, whose obverse was danger and evil. The words from *Macbeth* leapt into his thoughts, conjured up from some deep-seated awareness that all was far from well: 'By the pricking of my thumbs something wicked this way comes.' He was right to feel uneasy. Murder had been committed. But where there was murder, there had to be a solution. In his experience there were very few unsolved crimes.

Someone, somewhere, always held the vital clue. What could account for his sense of imminent disaster? Everything possible had been set in motion to track down the killer.

Police constables had been alerted to make discreet inquiries from neighbours and tradesmen around the region of Miss Errington's house and details of any suspicious circumstances or persons would be reported back to him.

Two days later he awoke to a hammering on his front door. He heard Mrs Brook's protesting voice and instinct told him that the call was urgent and that he was needed.

Jumping out of bed he stared over the banister into the agitated face of PC Dean looking up at him from the hall below.

'There's been another murder, sir. Another woman— '

'Where?' shouted Faro, already pulling on his clothes.

'Coffin Lane again, sir. Just a few yards from where we found the first one.'

Chapter Seven

Five minutes later, Faro and Vince were in Coffin Lane.

As they stared down at the second victim, they were joined by Conan, whom PC Dean had met on his way to the surgery, returning from a difficult confinement.

Vince paused in his brief examination, looked up at them and shook his head. 'Stabbed in the chest. The wound proved fatal almost instantaneously.' He gestured towards the centre of the lane. 'I reckon he grabbed her – over there – stuck the knife in her and then dragged her body over here to the side of the road for concealment in a snowdrift. There hasn't been any more snow and there are smears of blood across the road.'

The snow was too hard-packed for anything as useful as footprints; there were just two faint indentations a short space apart which suggested the heels of some inert figure had been dragged towards the snowdrift.

'When did it happen?' Faro asked Vince as he completed his brief examination of the body.

'More than twelve hours ago. Say, eight o'clock last night – would you agree, Conan?'

'Almost certainly. The police surgeon will doubtless confirm that.'

The mortuary carriage arrived. The two doctors departed fearing that they had a line of patients in the waiting-room, leaving Faro to accompany the corpse.

With Jim Dean at his side he did his best to appease the constable's curiosity without giving too many indications of his present line of thought, or the serious and sensational indications of this new and gruesome discovery.

'Is this a random killing, sir? Do you think there's some connection between the two of them?'

'I have no idea, Constable,' said Faro honestly.

He went down into the police mortuary praying that this was not some unknown woman and that there would be a link between the two killings.

This time the victim looked slightly better off than Molly. Her clothes were a pathetic bundle lying on a trestle beside her, but they did not look like a servant's clothes: the navy blue serge costume was of good quality, as were her hat and gloves.

There was no darned underwear or stockings. Although she had lain in the snowdrift all her linen looked fresh-laundered. There was a gold brooch and a wedding ring, a pair of fairly new boots and one patent shoe, which had presumably fallen out of the basket she was carrying.

He recalled Conan picking it up and looking round for the missing partner.

Dr Craig beamed at Faro. 'Same weapon as was used on the first victim, Inspector,' he said triumphantly. 'Could be the identical knife.'

That was one possible link, thought Faro hope-fully, as he asked, 'Any identification?'

'Indeed yes. Here! This was in her outside pocket.'

Another letter, but this time addressed to Mrs Ida Simms in Briary Road, Glasgow.

Faro skimmed the contents. It was signed 'Yours affectionately, Mary Fittick' and the notepaper was headed 22 The Villas, Musselburgh.

It appeared that Mrs Ida Simms was coming on a long-awaited visit to her friend and for the first time, since there were precise directions from the railway station at Waverley to the Pleasance where she would take the train from St Leonards to Musselburgh.

'Fortunately for us, she didn't commit all these directions to memory,' he said.

But what had led her to continue her journey past the station to Coffin Lane?

He took a carriage to St Leonards where he was in luck. The Musselburgh train was just about to leave. He decided to interview Mrs Fittick and fully expected that she would reveal some link with her friend and the murder of Molly Blaith.

Staring out of the window at the snow piled by the side of the line on the single-track railway, he was suddenly hopeful.

Until the meeting with Mrs Fittick, he pushed deliberately to the back of his mind the idea that this was a random killing and that they had some kind of a maniac to deal with.

The snow was even worse in Musselburgh, the roads mere tracks of brown slush, but at last he found his way to The Villas where a plump, pleasant-looking woman in her mid-forties opened the door to him.

Her look of surprise changed to one of horror when he introduced himself, and producing the letter she had written to her friend, explained that Mrs Simms had met with a fatal accident.

'Oh, how awful. I can't believe it. Poor dear Ida. She's always so careful about everything. It's this terrible weather. She must have slipped and fallen— '

Alerted by her weeping, a younger version of the distraught woman rushed in and put a consoling arm around her.

'I'm Tina – her sister. What's all this about?'

As Mrs Fittick sobbed out that poor Ida was dead, Tina's angry, reproachful look in Faro's direction said quite pointedly that the whole thing was his fault.

These were the times he hated most, having to break such news to family or friends. He had never had the heart for it. It sickened him, although other detectives in his senior bracket had no such compunction about handing over this worst part of the whole sordid crime business to some unfortunate constable.

At last Mrs Fittick dried her eyes and sought to regain her composure. The letter Mrs Simms had carried lay on the table between them and Tina said, 'I have never met Ida, but Mary has talked about her for years. She was from Glasgow like us.' And with a compassionate sigh, 'They were best friends.'

Mary put aside her handkerchief, straightened her shoulders, ran a hand across her hair. 'Make us a cup of tea, Tina, there's a good lass.'

'You'll be all right?'

'Of course I will. It's just the shock of it all.'

As Tina departed, Mary Fittick took a deep breath between a sigh and a sob. 'Poor Ida. She was just coming on a visit. We used to work together in the factory. We hadn't met for oh, years, it must be, and not since poor Ida lost her man in a railway accident and she had to go out to work to make ends meet.

'He hadn't left her comfortably off, ye ken. Bit of a drinker, he was, but good enough to her otherwise. Anyways, she hadn't had a break for years and now,' she added breathlessly, 'when I think how I was always writing to her, persuading her to come to Edinburgh, telling her how grand it would be for her to have a change of scene and a proper wee holiday— '

Remembrance was too much. 'Oh, oh – I could kick myself, really I could. If only I'd left well alone, she'd still be alive— '

Sobs threatened for a moment, then straightening her back with effort, she said, 'I was just remembering how angry I was when she didn't arrive. Oh, I wish I hadn't been fuming, but anyone would, waiting at the Pleasance for an hour in that awful weather. It gets dark early and I was getting scared. You know, this woman we read about being murdered. And I started wondering whether I'd walk up to Waverley, whether she'd missed the train or got the day wrong.'

She sighed. 'I'd decided at the last minute to surprise her, take the train to St Leonards and meet her. You know what it's like when someone doesn't turn up, you're torn between anxiety and anger at being kept waiting. And I was frozen. When the last train for Musselburgh arrived I had to take it. I told the guard if he saw anyone like my friend waiting around to tell her. I felt terrible then and now I feel much worse than terrible, when I think of sitting in that train with my wicked thoughts.' She stopped and looked at Faro. 'Carriage accident, was it?'

Faro nodded vaguely. 'You say she had no other friends in Edinburgh, no contacts?'

Mrs Fittick seemed to think this an odd question but she shook her head. 'No, she's hardly been out of Glasgow in her life before and this was to have been her first sight of Edinburgh. Oh, she was looking forward to that.'

'You mentioned that her husband was killed in an accident. Did they have any family?'

Mrs Fittick pursed her lips. 'Only the one lass and they never got on well. Miss High and Mighty, Ida called her. Oh, she did well for herself, went to work in a big house and married her boss, a wealthy old man three times her age.'

She sniffed disapprovingly. 'Once she had money and a social position Ida felt that she didn't want her poor ma and da any more and that was why Mr Simms took to the drink. She came to his funeral, though. Things might have got better between her and her ma except that Ida didn't like her second man either.'

She paused and Faro said gently: 'She will have to be told. Do you have an address?'

Mrs Fittick shook her head. 'I do not. But I dare say Ida's neighbour could tell you. They were very friendly – she'll be shocked to hear this terrible news— '

Before leaving he had to tell her the truth was even more terrible than she had thought: her friend had been attacked and stabbed in Coffin Lane.

He left her being consoled by her young sister, assuring them, although it was cold comfort, that her killer would be found and brought to justice.

He returned to Edinburgh very thoughtfully having decided that informing the daughter wasn't a job he would delegate to the Glasgow City Police after all. He would go himself tomorrow, sum up the situation and talk to Ida's neighbour, although he was doubtful that would yield any clues to the murderer's identity.

Were there too many coincidences about these cases? And why should the two women have both been killed in Coffin Lane within yards of each other?

Almost against his will he remembered its evil history, how once on the city outskirts it had earned its name from the gibbet that was used to hang criminals, political and otherwise.

Murderers and highwaymen were carried out in carts to be strung up, their last earthly vision the heights of Arthur's Seat, their sightless eyes picked out by ravens as flesh rotted in chains until the bones fell apart and shared dust with the earth beneath.

Coffin Lane it became when the suburbs of Newington sprang up; presumably the nearness of a small burying ground conjured up less gruesome imaginings for the owners of those handsome villas.

But the change of name could do little to alter a bad reputation, of hanged men and the ghost of a sixteenth-century witch. Drowned in St Mary's Loch, she had died with a curse on her lips.

Faro shook his shoulders as if to free himself from such morbid imaginings. Two women murdered. The murderer had succeeded with the second killing although the first victim had not died immediately but, what was perhaps worse, had bled to death alone in the snow.

Whoever committed such crimes was no spectre of Arthur's Seat, but someone real enough to kill.

Vince and Conan were waiting for him at the house. They listened to Mrs Fittick's story with an air of expectancy which he doused by shaking his head.

Vince nodded eagerly towards Conan: 'You'd better tell him.'

Conan shrugged. 'I would very much like to find the missing shoe – remember the patent slipper that I saw lying near the woman's body?'

'I presumed that it had fallen out of the basket she was carrying,' said Faro.

Vince and Conan exchanged glances. 'That's what we thought too. After surgery we went back and searched. But we couldn't find the matching one,' said Conan.

'And we did our own bit of detective work. The woman was wearing boots, as you'll remember.'

'That was easy, Vince. No one would wear slippers in snowy weather like this,' said Conan.

'Wait a moment. She was going on a visit, she might have carried them to change into,' said Faro.

'Except that the slippers were far too small for her,' said Conan triumphantly. 'Didn't you notice the size of her boots?'

And Faro hadn't noticed. One of his weaknesses was that he was notoriously unobservant when it came to women's wearing apparel.

As a married man of some years, Conan doubtless had expertise in such matters while Faro had missed the significance completely.

Now he remembered the stout but petite Mrs Fittick. 'Then they probably were a present for her friend.'

'What about this missing knife? The police surgeon believes the same weapon was used in both cases,' said Vince. 'I wonder if our murderer carried it away.'

The same kitchen knife, thought Faro. Were the doctors aware of the horrifying significance? That both victims had been killed by the same hand?

'Could be out there anywhere, Vince,' said Conan. 'Hidden by snow, it'll probably turn up when the thaw sets in.'

'But too late to be of any use in this investigation,' said Faro, gloomily aware that the missing knife was the first and only clue, the one vital link that might somehow lead him to the killer's identity.

If he could find it.

Returning from the Central Office later that evening, Faro walked in on one of the frequent disagreements between Vince and Olivia over a proposed visit to Solomon's Tower.

Kate had mentioned that her uncle would most cordially welcome them for a family Christmas dinner. Olivia had greeted this invitation with enthusiasm and already that afternoon, she and Kate had been discussing the provision of food.

Mrs Brook, also consulted, had glowed with pleasure at the idea of yet another banquet.

'It's a brilliant idea,' said Olivia. 'Quite a romantic setting too, especially since Kate has done so much to the interior. Rose will love it.' But this reference to his adored young half-sister failed to tempt Vince to change his mind.

'I don't think it's a good idea at all,' was his sullen response.

'Come along, dear, it is Christmas. It must be years and years since the old gentleman had such an opportunity. I doubt if he even remembers the last time.' She paused. 'After all he is Kate's uncle, all the family he has,' she reminded him gently, 'and we cannot deprive him of the chance to share in our celebrations— '

'You're not exactly wringing my heartstrings,' Vince interrupted. 'I don't see— '

'But then, my love, you never do,' Olivia cut in shortly. 'It would be exceedingly rude to Conan and Kate. And it is to be in his house, not ours.'

She paused, and regarding Vince's stony face, put a gentle hand on his arm. 'We don't have to ask him here, even presuming he would be willing to come, but Kate is doing so much at the Tower. She is such a good soul – they both are – and the party will be such a treat for the old gentleman.'

'You go then, and take Jamie, I have no objections to that,' said Vince huffily.

'No, dear. You must come. I insist, and it would be churlish to refuse,' said Olivia sharply. Her husband's quite unreasonable dislike for Sir Hedley was one of the few disagreeable facets of his character with which she had completely failed to come to terms.

'Besides,' she said helplessly to Faro as Vince stalked out of the room, 'I am fond of Sir Hedley. He's all that's left of a bygone age. I can't understand Vince's behaviour, really I can't.'

She looked at Faro as if he might be able to provide the answer. 'There must be some very good reason, dear Vince is so rational about everything normally. What on earth makes him behave in this – unfortunate manner? Did they quarrel?'

'No, my dear. And I am as much in the dark as you are. From their first meeting when Sir Hedley wanted so much to be on good terms – that was extraordinary in itself, since he has always been such a recluse – Vince just couldn't abide him, could hardly be civil to him.'

Olivia sighed. 'You know, I expect that he almost turned down Conan's application just because of the relationship with Kate.'

'I'm glad you talked him out of that, my dear. He would have lost the services of an excellent doctor.'

'I do agree. I've hoped since Kate and I are such friends, and because her uncle dotes on wee Jamie, that Vince's heart might soften towards him. But no—' She held up her hand as Vince's footsteps approached. As he came in she sneezed violently. 'Oh dear, I seem to be taking a wretched cold.'

Vince hovered anxiously, put a hand on her forehead. 'You don't seem feverish, but you must take care.'

'It's just a sniffle, dear. Kate gave me some of Conan's magic drops to take at bedtime.'

'What are they?'

'A prescription of his own invention.'

Vince looked interested. 'I must get it from him. We are desperate for remedies for patients with colds and it might help us handle this influenza epidemic.'

Olivia didn't appear at breakfast and to Faro's anxious enquiry, Vince said, 'She had a poor night, feeling queasy. I thought she'd better have a morning in bed. Nanny will keep Jamie out of her way. We don't want him catching anything. If it's influenza then we are all susceptible. It could spread through the house,' he said gloomily.

And as Faro prepared to leave he said, 'I trust you are feeling quite fit, Stepfather. You're looking quite tired these days.'

'I am in perfect health, thank you,' said Faro icily and departed hurriedly.

He did not welcome another of Vince's lectures on slowing down. There were enough people commenting on his approach to fifty to make him feel unreasonably ancient.

And he was getting very sensitive to that particular subject, especially as he had enough to do keeping all his wits about him and in maintaining the stamina necessary to solve two murders.

He was not prepared for an attack on a third woman.

Chapter Eight

The killer's third victim was still alive when she ran out of Coffin Lane and collapsed on Dalkeith Road, her jacket torn and blood oozing on to the road from a stab wound in the chest.

With great presence of mind one of the horrified onlookers remembered there was a doctor's surgery close by and that Inspector Faro lived in Sheridan Place.

About to depart for the Glasgow train, by the time Faro reached the scene, PC Dean was already lifting the injured woman into a carriage. Whereas the constable looked anxious and stricken, Dr Spens hovered importantly, giving directions.

He beamed on Faro. 'Glad to see you, sir. This is a hospital case.'

'I'll come with you.'

'They were very fortunate that I was just setting foot in the street . . .' Angus prattled on about Vince and Conan not having arrived yet and how many patients they would have to deal with that morning without his assistance.

He never once glanced at the white face opposite, but there was no problem about identification this time. Faro knew her.

Her name was Rita, a local prostitute who plied her trade in the region of the railway at St Leonards. She was frequently to be seen talking to prospective clients around the inns near the Pleasance and according to the police she had recently extended her activities further afield to include the prosperous villas of Newington and Priestfield.

Rita knew all about public probity and private vice and the lusts that lay behind the modestly curtained windows in the hearts of their respectable owners.

She was very discreet. No one at first glance would have recognised the hallmark of her trade, for she was quietly dressed and gently spoken, as befitted a woman from the Highlands.

Since there had been no outcry, no outraged complaints from the residents, she had introduced the less outrageous of her colleagues, 'girls' who were careful and shrewd in choosing their targets. Until they made some fatal mistake of opportuning some high-minded moral gentleman who felt it was his bounden duty to complain, policemen like PC Dean would continue to turn a blind eye on the existence of Rita.

Ignoring the law that said soliciting was illegal, they would continue to exchange cordial greetings and politely pass the time of day when they met.

Rita was a cheery soul, not in the least vulgar, and wiser policemen like Faro had long recognised that the Ritas of this world, like themselves, had to find means of making a living. Society was responsible, and whether they liked it or whether it was repugnant to them, selling their bodies in order to survive was often a necessity, especially if there were children.

Many had children and were good caring mothers, who regarded prostitution as a means of putting bread in their mouths and keeping them out of the dreaded orphanages.

Faro was well acquainted with Rita and the conditions of her life. She had been working the district for several years now since she first came to Edinburgh, a pretty young Highland girl with an illegitimate infant to support.

He had sympathy for her, knowing that but for a fateful meeting long ago with a young policeman called Jeremy Faro, such might well have been the fate of Lizzie Laurie and her wee Vince might have had a very different future.

Although Rita was still alive, Faro was angry; sad and angrier than he had been at the deaths of the first two victims. If he could have laid hands on the killer at that moment, he would have done him considerable violence and would cheerfully have included Angus Spens, whose self-importance had revealed callous indifference to the murdered women.

'She must have been pretty desperate to trudge out in the snow,' Jim Dean said sympathetically. 'Not much business at the railway in this weather, I suppose.'

'Business?' That attracted Spens' attention. He stared at the unconscious woman in disgust. 'You mean she is – a – a prostitute. Well, well, that sort of creature usually gets what she deserves.'

Before Faro or Dean could comment, the police carriage turned on to the main road where Conan had just arrived at the surgery door.

Faro leaped out. 'We have another victim. She's still alive.'

'Hospital case? Very well, I'll come with you. A moment while I leave a message for Vince.'

He reappeared with dressings to staunch the blood. There was nothing else he could do.

At Faro's anxious glance, he shook his head and silently they watched over her on the short distance to the hospital. There they waited while Conan, giving brief instructions, had her wheeled into the ward.

At last he emerged. 'She's still alive. Same knife wound, I'm afraid. And I wouldn't be surprised if the same weapon was used again.'

'Serious?'

'She's lost a lot of blood, she's very badly shocked but hopefully she'll survive.'

'And be able to tell us something about this madman when she recovers consciousness,' said Faro grimly. 'I'll wait.'

Conan looked at him. 'It may be some time, sir.'

'Very well. Dean can stay with you.'

Conan nodded. 'We'll send for you as soon as she is able to talk.' He smiled wanly and gave Faro a little shove. 'Go on, sir. You look exhausted. When did you last eat?'

Faro shrugged. 'Sometime today. Breakfast I think. Or was it last night?'

Conan took him firmly by the arm, steered him towards the door. 'Home, sir. Or I'll have Mrs Brook to reckon with.'

*

But Faro had no intentions of returning home: his feelings of urgency dictated that he stay in the vicinity of the hospital.

A tavern two streets away provided him with enough nourishment, a pie and a pint of ale, to satisfy the appetite, but somewhat less than the satisfaction of Mrs Brook's pleasant meals.

Half an hour later, he was running upstairs to the ward where Rita lay, pale as death itself.

Conan was there with Dean.

'Well, what news?'

'She's alive and she's given us a description of her attacker, sir.'

'Well?' said Faro.

The two men exchanged glances. 'You'll find this hard to believe, sir,' said Dean.

'Try me!'

'Our killer is a woman, sir.'

Chapter Nine

Conan indicated the motionless figure in the bed. 'She's still asleep,' he whispered. 'Given her laudanum. Go on, Constable. Tell the inspector.'

'It was like this, sir— '

But before Dean could continue, Rita heard their voices. Opening her eyes, she groaned and tried to sit up.

Conan went over. Feebly she pushed him aside. Pointing to the little group at the bedside, recognising only the policeman, she sobbed, 'It was a woman stabbed me, Constable. A woman wearing one of those poke bonnets, old-fashioned, like my ma wore.' Her eyes widened in horror. 'She ran towards me. I thought she was lost, wanted directions, or something. I stopped and she just stuck this great knife in me.'

Her face white, she clutched her chest and dropped back to the pillows. The duty nurse, hearing the commotion, pushed them aside. Taking Rita's pulse, she said sternly, 'I think you'd better leave, gentlemen. Come back later.'

In the corridor, Faro stopped. 'Remain with her, Constable.' And to Conan: 'Only a madwoman would fit the bill. Frenzied attacks to maim rather than kill.

If our first victim had been on the game then there might have been more reason: outraged wife – that sort of thing.'

Conan looked thoughtful. 'True. Clearly she has no idea where to strike effectively to kill in that moment of madness.' He bit his lip and said slowly, 'A madwoman. It makes sense.'

'From the asylum, you mean,' said Faro.

Conan sighed. 'Alas, yes. And unless I am mistaken perhaps one of my own patients.'

At Faro's horrified exclamation, he nodded. His voice urgent, he added, 'Would you care to accompany me, sir?'

'What are we waiting for? We can do no good here.'

Dean was sent for a carriage and while they waited, Faro said, 'You already knew, didn't you? That the killer might be a woman. Something to do with those slippers, was it?'

Conan smiled. 'You amaze me.'

'I should have worked it out for myself. You were so damned drawn to that one patent slipper that you got Vince to go back with you and search for the other. And then the size was wrong.' Faro sighed heavily. 'I was listening, instead of thinking. You know who it is, I gather?'

Conan drew a deep breath. 'I know who it *could* be – who it could have been, given her former history. I just hope that I am wrong.'

'Indeed? Violent was she— ?'

'Forgive me, sir,' Conan interrupted. 'I'd rather say no more until we talk to the matron at the asylum.'

*

Faro looked out of the window. 'This isn't the way to the asylum – we're going towards Morningside.'

'Right, sir,' said Conan. 'Summerhill Home, a very special asylum. They prefer to call it an institution for distressed patients. It's for the rich, who can be kept safely under lock and key at their family's expense and discretion.'

Faro felt relieved that it was not the bedlam he feared as they turned into the gates of a large house concealed from the road by high walls and a large number of trees.

The gardens were extensive. Pleasant lawns with magnificent views over the Pentland Hills suggested a harmonious setting for summer afternoon teas under shady trees.

The vestibule where they waited to be received by the matron was refreshingly ordinary and not much different at first glance from the threshold of any family mansion.

The matron greeted Conan affably, like an old friend. 'Good to see you, Dr Pursley. I'm afraid Lady Celia isn't here at the moment—'

Interrupted by Conan who introduced Inspector Faro, the matron had the unlikely name of Miss Smiles, which fitted her pleasant cheerful countenance, comfortable figure and warm handshake.

She turned back to Conan. 'She isn't in her room, Doctor, so I'm afraid there will be no pleasant afternoon walk for her today.'

'Where is she?' asked Conan.

'Oh dear!' The smiling face turned grave. 'We really don't know, exactly. I'm afraid she went out on one of her usual expeditions and failed to return.'

'When was this?'

'I'm not sure for certain – perhaps two or three days ago,' was the unhappy response.

There was an explosion of anger from Conan. 'All that time you knew one of your patients was missing and you did nothing.' He gave Faro a helpless look.

'Is this important, Inspector?' Miss Smiles addressed Faro, her worried expression confirmation of the gravity of his visit. Without awaiting his response, she nodded. 'I see. Dr Pursley comes in regularly,' she said. 'He called in on Monday, just after she had left.' Turning to him reproachfully, she added, 'You were informed then that she had gone out.'

'Of course. I remember now.'

'On her own?' queried Faro.

'Yes.'

'I find that somewhat surprising. Is it usual?' demanded Faro of Conan.

'Let me explain,' said Conan wearily. 'Celia wasn't in her room when I went upstairs. On a fine day we walk in the grounds together. I talk to her, get her to talk to me – about the past. That's the best possible treatment— '

'Dr Pursley's treatment has been excellent,' the matron interrupted and turning to him she said gently, 'You know quite well, Doctor, we have instructions from you in the matter, that she is on no account to be made to feel like a prisoner. That to be kept locked up, under restraint, could completely destroy all your progress with her.'

And turning to Faro, 'May I be told what all this is about, Inspector? Has she stolen something again?'

'Again!'

At his puzzled exclamation, she nodded. 'She can be rather light-fingered from time to time. Occasionally she sees something in a shop and brings it back with her, forgetting, of course, that such items must be paid for. Rest assured, if there has been a complaint to you, the shopkeeper will be reimbursed by us.'

'It is more serious than that, Miss Smiles,' interrupted Conan. 'She has – attacked passers-by,' he ended lamely.

Miss Smiles frowned. 'How extraordinary. She has not shown any symptoms of violence all the years she has been with us— ' Pausing she frowned. 'Except for one small incident in the kitchen – over a burnt roast – when she attacked a fellow patient with a knife. That was some time ago; since then, nothing. In fact, she has become a model patient under Dr Pursley's care.'

She smiled at him. 'Indeed yes, a trusted member of our little community.' And to Faro: 'As Dr Pursley has perhaps told you, she has been well educated.'

'That is so,' Conan explained. 'Celia comes of a titled family although they would not care to admit that she exists any more, the punishment for throwing herself into the lake with her newborn child. The baby drowned and when she was dragged out she tried to murder one of her kinsman, so a trust fund was set up to pay the fees for her residence as far away as possible. When she was admitted to Summerhill as a patient, they were careful to give out publicly that she had died of typhoid while on holiday in Italy and because of the strict measures regarding

75

epidemics, her body could not be returned to Britain. She was allegedly buried near Florence.'

He shook his head. 'Celia's is a tragic case, a prime example of the gross mishandling of a woman's life by her family. As matron knows, this is one of the cases that I have been investigating, trying to put right a wrong after so many years.'

A sniff from Miss Smiles indicated that his faith was a little in question and looking at her sharply, Conan continued, 'My resolve is unshaken. I am determined to prove that insanity is a sickness of the mind, especially to a woman after the suffering involved in concealing the birth of an unwanted child. With understanding, care and the right treatment I believe it can be cured, the patient returned to society fully healed, a respectable, reliable citizen.'

'Much of what Dr Pursley says is admirable and is certainly true regarding Lady Celia,' said the matron. 'She has never shown the least sign of derangement, as I've told you. Distress, and sorrow, naturally, but such emotions have responded to medical care, and the administration of a little harmless laudanum has been sufficient to put her to rights again.'

She sighed. 'Personally I enjoy her company. She is bright and intelligent and I look forward to our occasional walks together in the gardens. I assure you, sir, it's a tonic after dealing with the needs of some of our more desperate patients.'

As an afterthought she added somewhat reluctantly, 'True, she has a rather bad temper at times – but the laudanum helps to quiet her. A wildness sometimes seizes her, the desire for self-destruction— '

'Particularly at the full moon, is that not so, matron?' Conan put in.

'Indeed. But her anger is against herself, rather than against others, as if at such times she realises the injustice of her virtual imprisonment and banishment from the world outside.'

She shrugged. 'But, gentlemen, if we were to put away behind locked doors everyone who lost their patience from time to time, then we would have most of the population behind bars – and I include myself,' she added with a little laugh.

With a look at the doctor, she continued, 'We were assured that her violent past when she drowned her newborn child and attacked her family with a kitchen knife was far behind her. Such days are happily long forgotten. Or so she has cleverly led us to believe,' she added anxiously.

Again she turned to Faro. 'We have put her in charge of our little library, Inspector. We even allow her to go into town unaccompanied. And she has always – always returned.'

'Until this particular Monday,' said Conan sternly.

Miss Smiles sighed. 'When she didn't put in an appearance at teatime we presumed that Dr Pursley had met up with her in the grounds.' She looked at him, made a helpless gesture.

'And so you allowed her to disappear,' said Conan slowly. 'And when did you discover she was missing?'

'Not until Thursday evening, I'm afraid.'

'When she had been missing for three days!' exclaimed Conan. 'Then why didn't you notify me –

you know the rules about getting in touch with someone of authority in such cases. Anything might have happened to her,' he added indignantly.

'I assure you we would have done so in the normal way but with the weekend intervening – many of our staff have their time off then – and of course, this outbreak of influenza among the nurses has left us severely short-staffed.'

And inefficient, thought Faro grimly as she continued, 'As you know, Doctor, Lady Celia spends most of the day on her own with her books.'

She looked across at Faro appealingly. 'She isn't supervised in any way, Inspector. She has free access to the kitchen to prepare her own meals if she wishes and we don't look in every night to lock her in her room. Such behaviour would be unthinkable. In her case since she trusts us and has come to regard this as her true home, it would upset her dreadfully and destroy all Dr Pursley's good work.'

When Conan didn't respond, she sighed. 'I am exceedingly sorry, Doctor, we seem to have made a genuine mistake, but the thought that she might have been contemplating running away from us did not seem possible. She seemed – well, happy.' And as an afterthought, 'Where could she go? She had never more than a few coins in her possession.'

She glanced at Faro. 'I can only presume by your presence here, Inspector, that we have some cause for genuine alarm. In this incident – these attacks on passers-by – I trust no one was severely injured. We will, of course, recompense any material damage.'

Faro pretended not to hear that. 'Was there anyone

she might have visited in Edinburgh on a regular basis, where she may have made friends?'

Miss Smiles shook her head. 'She always kept very much to herself. That is not difficult in this environment,' she added desperately. 'There are few patients who would be on her intellectual level, and their condition makes them very suspicious. The fact that she was liked by – and a favourite with – some of the staff made them feel she was in league against them. In fact, to be honest, most of them were afraid of her.'

Glancing towards the window, she laughed uneasily. 'I would even see them cower as she passed by or if she went to sit at their table during meals, they would seize their plates and sit elsewhere, trying to avoid her shadow. That was one reason why we allowed her free access to the kitchen.' Again that troubled glance. 'Some of our more disturbed patients believed that she had occult powers— '

'A witch, you mean?' said Faro.

'Something of the sort. Such happenings are distressing for everyone concerned.' Miss Smiles looked thoughtful. 'You asked about friends; well, there is a person who might fit that category. An antiquarian bookshop on the High Street owned by an old gentleman, an ordained minister now retired. Celia once hinted to me that she had known him from her childhood days in Argyll. He may even have tutored in her own family.

'She might well have gone to visit him. Very likely indeed,' she added triumphantly. 'Dr Benjamin lends her books on Scottish history and the classics.'

When Faro looked surprised at her choice of literature, Miss Smiles went on, 'She even borrows and obtains books some of the staff would like to read. Dr Benjamin used to visit us and bring his books once upon a time, that is how they met again. But in the last year or two he has been crippled by rheumatism and has difficulty making the long journey. They have become friends and he specially asked if he could see her now and again. He wasn't worried by her past, said she had a fine mind and, indeed, he shared Dr Pursley's opinion that her incarceration in an – institution for half a lifetime was a miscarriage of justice.'

Conan laughed. 'Doesn't that prove I was right, matron? You have a scholar's backing as well as a medical man's.'

In the hall a clock melodiously chimed four and a bell shrilled through the hall. There was movement of scampering feet above their heads.

Miss Smiles rose from her desk. 'Gentlemen, I must leave you.' And with a helpless gesture towards Faro, she repeated, 'Is all this a matter of vital importance? You still haven't told me what has happened,' she reminded him.

'It's a police matter, madam. You'll hear the details in due course. Meanwhile, if you would be so good as to give Dr Pursley this bookseller's address.'

Leaving Conan to evade the matron's question as tactfully as he could with a vague nod and a request to let him know immediately if the missing woman returned, Faro strolled to the front door to wait outside for Conan who joined him shortly afterwards.

Watching Faro's expression, Conan said unhappily, 'I can make a shrewd guess at your thoughts, sir.'

'Can you indeed?'

'You are thinking we may have let a killer out on society. And I'm not blaming you. I had been warned, but I thought I knew best,' he added bitterly. 'The problems with this sort of violent condition is that patients can appear – and actually be – quite normal for years. Then something, perhaps a word remembered, a phrase or a scene from the past, triggers off a chain of thoughts and memories and hurls them back into the abyss again. I should have taken into account that Celia is at an unfortunate age for women—' He shook his head. 'Trouble is, I should have guessed from that patent slipper if we had heard that she was missing. No one but Celia would go out in such weather so inadequately clad. But she was vain about her small pretty feet and abhored boots, even in winter.'

He sighed. 'I blame myself, sir. I thought I was doing the right thing, encouraging Summerhill to treat her as a normal person. Now I find we have a very serious situation on our hands. With this kind of brain disorder, about which we still know very little indeed, it appears that the lust to kill anyone without cause or reason can recur. And once they taste blood, as one might say, it gets worse, they need more and more.'

Faro stopped walking. 'You are telling me that we have a killer, an indiscriminate killer who will put a knife in anyone who she regards as standing in her way?'

Conan nodded miserably. 'Yes. Literally – and that would seem to be the answer. What other is there?

Remember, of the three attacks only one has been a fatal stabbing.'

'But the first was still murder. Molly Blaith bled to death.'

'True. Fortunately the third one – Rita – is still alive.'

'Then we must find your missing patient at once. As long as she is at large she may well be tempted to add further victims to her list.'

Chapter Ten

Conan's revelations concerning the background of the missing woman left Faro a very unhappy man.

Time wasn't on his side, but then it never was, never had been. He knew it was vital that he track her down and put her behind bars before she attacked again.

Conan accompanied him to the Central Office and helped him to build up a complete description of Lady Celia for circulation in the district.

Going in search of the superintendent, Faro was vastly relieved to learn that he had not yet returned from a colleague's funeral in London.

His absence meant that Faro was in sole charge of the case. Accordingly he issued instructions that the woman's description be posted throughout the city with every constable in the district of Newington alerted. After wearying hours of combing the area around Arthur's Seat for evidence, at least they now knew who they were searching for.

In his long career Faro had investigated every aspect of murder, and in more than one case a woman had wielded the murder weapon, or more often slipped the arsenic into the unsuspecting cup. But never had he encountered a murder where the killer's identity was already known.

The hand holding the upraised knife to strike at random passers-by in this quiet suburb was that of a madwoman. A madwoman escaped from the institution where she had been incarcerated since she was sixteen years old.

Even Conan, who dealt with such tortuous matters as the intricacies of diseased human minds, had been lulled into believing her one deed of violence was an isolated occurrence and that her present state of mind was the result of injustice and long restraint. What he had failed to recognise was his patient's potential for breakdown and the gravity of what might then occur.

In considerable distress, he admitted to Faro that he had never given a second thought to the possibility that she might wish to escape from Summerhill, might even have plotted to take advantage of their trust in her to wreak revenge on the society which had assisted in depriving her of a lifetime's liberty. It was a terrible, vicious vengeance she sought on her own sex.

Faro felt sympathy for Conan, friend of those unfortunates behind locked doors, trying against all the odds to keep them from the horrors of insane asylums, trying to prove that violence was a sickness, a disease like any other. And for every disease Conan insisted science must provide a cure sooner or later.

If only it had been found in Lady Celia's case. According to Kate, he spent countless hours in the laboratory he had created for himself in Solomon's Tower, working endlessly with his cages of rats and mice, experimenting with drugs and devising new theories.

But even if he succeeded with animals, thought Faro, the human brain was a vastly more complex organ than that of a rodent.

At that moment, his own version of that elusive cure was more elementary. Find the madwoman and lock her up before more innocent citizens fell victim to the workings of her disordered brain.

He thought of women and girls in Newington going about their daily routines, absorbed by everyday problems of taking care of families, husbands, young children, parents, when suddenly from the dark shadows of Coffin Lane, a screaming virago with a knife launched herself upon them, stabbing, slashing—

His fears inevitably touched on his own home, and Mrs Brook, Olivia and Jamie's Nanny Kay. And in particular, Olivia's friend Kate who constantly travelled on foot between Sheridan Place and Solomon's Tower, her road taking her close by Coffin Lane.

And then there was his daughter Rose, soon to be arriving from Glasgow for Christmas. Should he suggest she cancel her visit? Knowing his brave Rose, he guessed she would treat such a suggestion with scorn.

He felt nervous, apprehensive, as never before in his career. He dare not rest or dream of relaxation until the mystery of the disappearance of the 'Lady Killer' (as the newspapers were to describe her) was solved.

But where to start?

He decided to return to the beginning.

On his way to the antiquarian bookshop, whose proprietor might or might not have news of Celia's whereabouts, he decided to revisit the scene of the crimes; Molly Blaith, who had bled to death under the snow, and Mrs Simms, who had been brutally murdered on her way to take the train to Musselburgh.

At least the third victim, Rita, still lived and perhaps she would have more valuable information by the time he returned to the hospital.

Coffin Lane was deserted. Snow lay upon snow, only a few depressed vestiges of hedgerow emerged from the drifts. A bitter wind blew from the direction of Arthur's Seat, a hollow chill eating into his bones.

He knew how carefully the area had been searched and that the vicinity where the bodies lay was unlikely to yield anything of significance until the thaw revealed perhaps too late a kitchen knife or a missing slipper.

He hurried back towards Minto Street past the scarlet mailbox emblazoned with the Queen's initials, 'VR', where Molly had failed to post her mistress's urgent letter to her solicitor.

He shook his head. Something nagged him about that interview with Miss Errington and as her house came into sight, he rang the bell and took a chance on her being at home and willing to see him.

His summons went unanswered but he was conscious of being watched and glancing quickly at the upstairs bow window, he saw a shadow that moved – a shadow wearing a lace cap and he was in time to glimpse a face quickly withdrawn as the curtain fluttered back into place.

He prepared to wait. It would obviously take her a little time to negotiate stairs unaided and by the time she appeared at the door in her wheelchair he was feeling cold and out of humour.

There was no maid in attendance and she greeted him with an impatience equal to his own.

'May I?' he asked and without awaiting her permission, he stepped boldly past her and into the hall.

Her lips tightened when he announced that there were a few questions covering one or two aspects of Molly's employment with her that he would like to clarify.

'If you would be so good— '

'Such as?' she interrupted. 'I have told you all I know about my companion.'

Companion now, was it? Again he was conscious of that lack of personal grief, the all-absorbing self-interest that made her regard Molly's horrific end as a personal inconvenience, a twist of fate sent personally to thwart her, to blight the smooth running of her everyday existence.

Or was indifference a screen for something more sinister?

'Would you be so good as to tell me exactly what happened as far as you can remember in those few minutes before Molly left the house to mail your letter?'

'I cannot recall anything unusual in her behaviour,' Miss Errington said stiffly.

Faro took out a notebook which she eyed with considerable disfavour. If he had made an improper gesture it could hardly have been less graciously received.

'I would like a list, as far as you are aware, of every tradesman with whom Molly would come into contact, or who calls at the house.'

The question raised an eyebrow. Pursing thin lips, she gestured with her hands. 'I have absolutely no idea about such matters, they are not of the slightest interest to me. Why on earth should you want such bizarre information?'

Faro suppressed a weary sigh. 'This is the usual procedure in murder investigations, madam. The information is circulated to our police constables who will pursue their inquiries most thoroughly by ascertaining if any of the tradesmen knew Molly or had friendly dealings with her.'

'Friendly, indeed!' was the shocked response. 'I cannot imagine Molly being acquainted with such – persons.'

Faro smiled wryly. 'Then I think you might be surprised to know how often servants confide in one another.'

'Confide,' she murmured as though the word conjured up more lurid visions than intimacy. 'And will such information help you track down whoever killed her?'

'That is the general assumption, madam. All such information gathered together can lead to evidence which will give us some indication of how our inquiries should proceed.'

She nodded assent, staring beyond him into the dark shadows beyond the stairs.

There was no more to be gained and Faro was relieved to shake off the aura of the house. Cold and gloomy in winter, he suspected it would not be greatly improved by summer, when sunlight became the aggressor, the enemy to be sternly held captive outside shuttered windows in case its invasion faded the worthless pictures, the tired fabrics of dreary furnishings.

'Inspector – here!'

A sibilant whisper came from beyond the railings. A face, Adie's face, looked up at him from the basement kitchen door.

'I've just got back. I was coming up to see if madam wanted tea 'cos she won't pay to have the bell fixed – and I heard what you were saying. So I stayed put.' She looked at him triumphantly. It was a look that he had recognised many times in the past. She had information.

'Well?'

'Just that she's an awful stickler for the truth, but she's no' telling it herself,' she added with a touch of malice. 'They had another awful row that day. Madam was always accusing her of thieving things and Molly was threatening to leave. She hinted that she had the offer of another job.'

Which accounted for the presence of that reference, thought Faro as Adie smiled delightedly at catching out her mistress in a lie.

Faro went away thoughtfully. A cripple defeated by disability and by life itself relying on a young active woman, living year after year in a cheerless atmosphere. A soul-destroying daily routine, the long hours of each day slowly ticking away on that asthmatic grandfather clock in the hall, with no other mortal save a kitchenmaid, set apart from them by her lower rung on the social scale.

He frowned, trying to remember. Was he missing some vital clue? Was it there in the house and he had overlooked it again? He considered Miss Errington, had noted that although her legs covered with a rug were undoubtedly fragile, her hands and arms were strong, as is often the case with invalids confined to wheelchairs.

Going down the path, he glanced at the upstairs window. Had it been Miss Errington in her white cap which concealed her hair? If so, if she was truly disabled, how had she negotiated that long flight of stairs unaided before getting into her wheelchair to greet him, if such a total lack of kindliness could be so called?

That bothered him. It might be significant, but not so significant, however, as the infernal red mailbox which loomed into view. Molly had walked straight past it with the letter in her hand, angry with Miss Errington after a blazing row. But why had she headed in the direction of Coffin Lane?

What on earth was she doing in that lonely spot on such a bitter evening? What had been her destination, or more likely, her assignation? He would have given much to know if her threat to find another situation was in earnest. Or was she secretly on the game too, he wondered, remembering Rita now recovering from shock.

True, in summer Coffin Lane took on the more benign aspect of a lovers' lane and the 'girls' were known to include it in their beat, wandering along in search of solitary clients from the golf course, with hopes of earning a quick shilling in the hedgerows at the base of Arthur's Seat. But clients would be unlikely to be tempted with four uncomfortable inches of hard-packed snow on the ground.

The mystery remained: what or who had enticed her to this deserted area?

There were two important questions still unanswered. If it wasn't Miss Errington he had glimpsed at the upstairs window, then who was she concealing? And more important, why?

That gave rise to a new possibility. Could Molly have been attacked before she left the house? Was that the reason for her disorientated flight? Was Adie's account just malice, or was there more to it? Now he imagined Molly running away terrified from someone in the house, someone angry, who had attacked her with the kitchen knife.

He shook his head, and pondering the imponderables, his footsteps led him back to the High Street, where he found to his annoyance that the antiquarian bookshop was closed.

There was no notice on the door but the thunder of the one o'clock gun from the castle ramparts reminded him that this was dinner time in Edinburgh. Rather than waste any more time, he decided to return to the hospital and see how Rita was progressing.

He was met by PC Dean, who had been on duty. His expression, grave and angry, told Faro more clearly than any words what to expect: 'Sorry, sir, she died an hour ago. Poor lass, poor lass.'

Chapter Eleven

Conan caught up with Faro as he was leaving the hospital.

'I'm on my way back to the surgery. Nothing I can do now.' He sighed. 'A sorry business.'

'Not what I expected to find,' said Faro.

Conan nodded. 'Nor I. The unknown factor – it appeared that she was an asthmatic. In the normal way she would have recovered, but the shock as well as the loss of blood sent her into a coma and killed her.' He paused. 'Your constable was quite shattered. It would seem he was on friendly terms with her. I didn't enquire whether that was in the line of business,' he added wryly. 'Seems that she lived by herself in one room in Fetters Close.'

'What about the child?'

Conan shook his head. 'Adopted a couple of years ago. Usual story, according to Dean. She felt it would be a better life for a wee girl never knowing the truth about her real mother.'

Outside, it was snowing again, the white purity of innocence speading a blanket over the evils of the day.

'I'm going back to the institution, to see if they

have any news of my missing patient,' said Conan grimly. 'What about you?'

Faro pointed towards the High Street. 'The anti-quarian bookshop, I think.'

Once again he found the shop closed. He tried the door leading to the flat above which he presumed might be the old man's residence.

There was no reply. Directly across the road was a tobacconist and snuff-seller's shop. A man who had been watching his activities with some curiosity through the window now came to the door.

'Dr Benjamin, you mean,' was the cheery response to Faro's enquiry. 'Came in two or three days syne for his baccy.' The man looked thoughtful. 'Mind you, sir, he was awfa' sniffly, didna' look great at all. I says to him: "Reckon you're coming down with the influenza." "Aye, you're right there, Bob." "Take to your bed, sir, and keep warm. That's always the best treatment. With a dram or two, ye'll be grand the morrow." "Aye, Bob," says he, "that's what I'll do." '

As he paused for breath, Faro seized the oppor-tunity to ask, 'And you haven't seen him since?'

Bob stared across the road. 'Not a sign of him. But that isn't unusual even when he's well. He keeps his own counsel.'

'What about the shop? Haven't there been cus-tomers enquiring?'

'He doesn't get many customers this time of year. Folk can do without books in this weather. Need to keep a good fire burning, keep cosy, like I told him. Well, well. I'd leave it for a day or two, he'll have taken to his bed. He'll be all right, strong as a horse, he is.' Turning he said, 'It'll be a book you're after, I suppose. If you'd like to leave a message, sir, I'll put it through the back door for him; he usually leaves it open.'

'I won't trouble you with that,' Faro said vaguely. 'I'll look in again when I'm passing.'

When he returned to the Central Office, Conan was waiting for him.

'I just missed you, sir. I walked past the shop – no, no news of Celia. Not a word. The shop was locked,' he said.

When Faro recounted his interview with the snuff-seller, Conan looked grave. 'If the old man is lying ill, then I think we should make it our business, considering the circumstances to, well, what you would call, force an entry.'

Faro smiled. 'I don't think that'll be necessary. The snuff-seller says the back door is kept open.'

Conan seized his bag, looked in and snapped it shut. 'Let's go, shall we? I had better have you with me, just in case.' He sounded anxious.

As they walked swiftly down the High Street Conan seemed preoccupied. Faro had spoken to him twice before he turned and said, 'Sorry, sir. It's just that I don't like this business. If this is where Celia used to go – and now she's disappeared and the old man hasn't been seen— ' He shook his head violently. 'I don't like it – I don't like the implications one bit.'

'Let's hope there is a perfectly innocent explanation.'

'You think so?' But Conan wasn't persuaded. 'Since Celia was last heard of visiting him a few days ago –

and we know she has attacked three women, and been responsible for the death of all of them, don't you think it's rather sinister?'

'This man was her friend, Conan. Why should she kill him?'

Conan shook his head. 'Violence breeds violence. Something inside her head has gone out of control, snapped. I hope the one thought predominant in my mind is not the right one,' he murmured as they approached the shop.

Across the road the snuff-seller's back was turned, as he talked animatedly to a customer. Unseen, they slipped down the close, then tapped on the back door.

There was no reply.

Opening the door they walked through the dark passage that led to the shop. On their left was a narrow stair.

They exchanged glances. Both recognised that curious unpleasant odour emanating from its direction as the smell of death, even before they found Dr Benjamin lying stiff and cold on the landing above.

Conan bent over him. 'He's been dead for several days, I'm afraid.'

Faro nodded. So much was painfully obvious. 'How did he die? What I'm asking is – did he die from the effects of influenza?'

Conan shook his head. 'We won't know that until we have a post mortem, but it has the appearance at first glance of natural causes. Thank God for that. I'd speculate that he developed pneumonia, aggravated by the neglected influenza.'

For the moment the missing woman was forgotten, then Faro sighed, remembering the reason for their concern.

'Now we'll never know whether she visited him or not.'

Conan straightened up. 'And we are no nearer discovering where she is hiding.' That was his main concern. 'I wouldn't have the foggiest notion where to begin looking for her.'

'Does she know where you live?'

Conan frowned. 'I may have mentioned to her that we were living in the city, out at Solomon's Tower. Yes, I think I did. But it's very doubtful if she'd remember or indeed if she knew where that was.'

'It's less than a quarter mile from Coffin Lane, Conan,' was Faro's grim reminder. 'Dr Benjamin might have told her. He would surely have street directories.'

It could be coincidence, on the other hand it might well account for the scene of the murders, if Celia was on the way to Solomon's Tower to find Dr Pursley. And each attack had been a few yards nearer.

So where could she be hiding now? And where would she strike next?

Both men, lost in their own thoughts, started when the back door opened and a voice shouted, 'Who's there? I saw you come in. What are you doing?'

Bob the snuff-seller hurried towards them. Suddenly he put his hand to his nose and raising his eyes from the body on the floor regarded them with a horrified expression.

'Is he dead then?' he whispered.

'I'm afraid so,' said Faro.

As Conan explained the circumstances of their

finding him, Bob said, 'You should have asked me first, he wouldn't want people coming in here unasked.'

As if it mattered now.

'Poor old Dr Ben. Such a fine man, and clever too. A great scholar.'

Faro had an idea. 'You are familiar with the bookshop, then?'

'I am that,' was the proud reply.

'Then while you're here perhaps you would like to look around the shop, see that everything is in order. Perhaps you would be so good as to lead the way.'

Bob stared at him doubtfully. 'What's all this about? What's your business, may I ask?'

'I'm a policeman,' said Faro, 'and until we know the exact circumstances of your friend's death— ' he indicated Conan: 'This gentleman is a doctor.'

'He's a bit late to be of any use. Dr Ben died of the influenza, we don't need a doctor to tell us what killed him,' was the indignant reply. 'We don't need to ferret about his shop to know that.'

Faro sighed. 'Believe me, sir, I know what I'm asking.'

Bob stared at them, horrified. 'You're thinking someone did him in, that's what.'

When Conan muttered a denial, Bob went on: 'If that's the way with it, they'll have me to deal with. Good kind old gentleman like him.'

'Please lead the way,' said Faro.

Bob was still murmuring under his breath about policemen and useless doctors as they followed him downstairs.

There was no obvious sign of disturbance.

'Where did he keep his money?'

'In the drawer on the desk there,' said Bob.

It was empty.

'He would carry his takings upstairs with him at the end of each day, I imagine. Like I do myself,' said Bob.

'Are you familiar with the contents of the shop?'

'Reasonably,' was the reply as he looked round the shelves apprehensively. 'I like a good book myself. And I know one when I see it. The old gentleman would recommend anything he thought would please me – mostly local history, and there have been some fine valuable ones passing through his hands from time to time.'

Bob turned to inspect the secretaire bookcase occupying one wall. Faro decided this was a delightful shop, one after his own heart. The smell of old leather and newsprint always fascinated him and he would have been happy to while away many an idle hour in such surroundings given happier circumstances.

'Over here, sirs,' called Bob from the direction of the glass-fronted bookcase. 'This is where he keeps his most valuable books.'

'Are you familiar with the contents? Would you know if there was anything missing?' asked Conan as the man inspected the shelves.

Suddenly Bob pointed to an empty space between two leather-bound books with faded spines. 'There, sirs. Gone from its usual place,' he said dramatically. 'That was his particular treasure. One of the first books ever printed about Edinburgh. I looked at it regularly. I was one of the privileged. He would hardly let anyone else handle it besides himself,' he said proudly.

Conan smiled. 'And did you know what this important book contained?'

Bob nodded eagerly. 'I do indeed, sir. It was all about the Templars and all the old legends. About treasure at Fast Castle and that old place at Arthur's Seat no one knows anything about – Solomon's House— '

'Tower,' Conan corrected him. 'And you're sure it's missing?'

'I am that, sir. Why, it was my favourite. Some rum old engravings it had in it. As I told you, I'm a bit of a historian myself and just the other week the old gentleman told me someone had been in to buy it. Keen as anything. He laughed about it. Said he'd been made a very substantial offer – two hundred guineas, something like that. And as the business hadn't been too good lately, I told him he was a mug to refuse it.'

He shook his head. 'But he was like that. He didn't like the look of the man, not one of his regulars, not even from these parts, he said. His books were his friends, precious to him as the children he never had. And he wasn't going to let it go to just anyone, not even for money. It belonged here in Edinburgh and he wasn't going to let it be taken away from its home.'

Faro called in the constable on the beat and arrangements were made for the police carriage to take Dr Benjamin to the hospital mortuary. The snuff-seller knew of no relatives.

Outside Conan said, 'At least it has nothing to do with the murders, thank heaven. Appearances suggest that the man died from natural causes – old age and pneumonia.'

While agreeing that Conan probably knew best, Faro would have liked to know more about the missing book. Had it been stolen by the man who wanted it so badly and refused to accept that it was not for sale? And if so, what was so important in the book that it necessitated a break-in? Was the burglary mere coincidence, occurring while the old man lay ill in bed upstairs, or had he disturbed the intruder who had then been responsible for his death?

Considering Faro's doubtful expression, Conan said, 'Alas, none of this brings us any nearer to finding Celia, does it?'

His voice urgent, he added, 'Time is of the essence now, sir. As long as she remains free – I am sure I don't have to tell you this – in her present mood of destruction no one is safe. We don't know where she is or when she might kill again.'

Chapter Twelve

The dramatic developments regarding the Lady Killer and the dead bookseller were the main topics of discussion at Faro's supper table that evening.

'We won't know for sure until after the post mortem whether the old man died as the result of some injuries that were not apparent or of pneumonia,' he told Vince. 'But it seems very unlikely that Conan's patient is involved.'

Vince nodded sympathetically. 'It's a terrible blow for him. His faith in his patients is touching, you know. He was so sure that she had been a victim of gross injustice all these years, that he was about to take on the full responsibility for her release.'

He paused, looking at Faro. 'Maybe he has told you this already? No?'

'Oh, then you don't know that he was trying to persuade Kate that they should have her to live with them at Solomon's Tower,' Olivia interrupted. 'She was not in the least keen about that – one eccentric person in the household was more than enough to contend with.'

'And she wasn't at all sure how the Mad Bart would react to having a woman living with them who had been declared mentally unstable, I am sure,' said Vince.

Olivia smiled. 'I can't see even our very sane Mrs Brook taking kindly to such an arrangement, can you? Nannies and maids who have all their faculties are considered unreliable in this house.'

Faro was surprised at Conan having made such a decision and he realised it explained a great deal about the doctor's reaction to recent events, his reluctance to admit that Celia knew where he lived, for instance.

Olivia, however, knew all about it. She was particularly concerned for Kate's possible involvement and she had some theories of her own.

'I think it is fairly obvious to Kate that Celia is in love with her doctor, absolutely obsessed by him.'

'My dear, she is old enough to be his mother,' Faro put in.

'And when has that made any difference to a sad and lonely woman falling in love with her doctor or her minister?' said Vince. 'It happens all the time.' Olivia looked quickly at him and he smiled. 'I haven't been in any danger personally but I could quote you chapter and verse on several cases, if I wasn't bound to secrecy.'

He paused. 'Of course Conan is far too modest to imagine such a situation. He thinks she regards him only as her saviour and protector.'

'You are inferring that such situations are fairly commonplace with susceptible women patients, even the well-balanced ones,' said Faro.

'Indeed. But for someone mentally disturbed— ' Vince shrugged eloquently.

'You're right, of course, and I should have thought of it,' said Faro. 'It explains some of the odd coincidences.'

'Such as?' queried Vince.

'Why all these attacks took place in Coffin Lane, on the road, one would say, to Solomon's Tower.'

'Wait a moment,' said Vince. 'You're suggesting that she was trying to get to Conan – and regarded these unfortunate women she met as rivals literally standing in her way— '

'I think we can get closer than that, lad. Let's suppose that, confused and lost, she asked them for directions. And when they did not know, or didn't reply, she imagined they were deliberately concealing Conan from her.'

'Yes, that's it. She was prepared to kill anyone who tried to keep her from her beloved doctor,' said Olivia triumphantly.

'If you are right and she had reached the Tower – and found Kate alone— ' whispered Vince in horrified tones.

'Now I know why Conan insists that Kate keeps the outer doors locked when she's alone there. I did think it odd at first seeing they are so isolated. But now – how awful!' said Olivia.

'You realise what this means,' said Vince. 'As long as this madwoman is loose, poor Kate is in terrible danger. Poor Conan. What a dilemma; not only must he feel a measure of guilt for those three women's horrific deaths but fear for Kate too.'

They were interrupted by Mrs Brook coming in to clear the supper dishes.

'Is there anything special you would like prepared for Miss Rose, Inspector?'

And Faro realised he had almost forgotten entirely that Rose was arriving the following day.

Faro awoke that morning feeling unusually happy.

Rose was coming for Christmas. He knew he shouldn't be glad that this was for her yet another Christmas apart from McQuinn, that she was still waiting for him to return from America.

As for Faro, he couldn't help being selfishly grateful for this extra time, the bonus of fate and McQuinn's determination that he must have a settled life to offer Rose before they married.

Rose would have resigned from her teaching situation and set off the next day on the first ship from Glasgow to New York if Danny had weakened, but he was utterly unshakeable in his purpose. He had not the least intention of letting her suffer the privations of a pioneering wife, especially as he was firmly resolved to move westwards, into that wild unknown territory where the law was only a figment of honourable men's imagination.

Lawless men and savage Indians. That was the picture he painted, but brave Rose, very much her father's child, was undaunted. She was very young still, not yet twenty and much younger than Danny, as he reminded her constantly. Telling her sternly that if she found someone else with a settled life, then she should forget all about him.

How she cried when she received his letter, but she kept her tears to herself, knowing that in his heart of hearts Pa would heartily agree with Danny for once.

It had taken him some considerable time to consider ex-Detective Sergeant Danny McQuinn, late of Edinburgh City Police, as good enough to be his daughter's husband and his son-in-law.

Faro had never been good at concealing the truth even from himself and Rose guessed that he would be relieved if she found a suitable husband and settled in Edinburgh or Glasgow for the rest of her life.

Such easy decisions were not for her. She knew and had known since she was a child when Danny McQuinn had saved her life in a kidnapping attempt, that he was her own, to be her one and only love. In that she never wavered, again showing that she was Faro's child, the daughter of his heart.

She often wondered if he worried as much about his other daughter, her younger sister Emily, happily married to an Orkney widower with good connections and an ancient lineage which had so gratified their grandmother, Mary Faro.

Emily had always been more conventional in her outlook than Rose, one reason why she and her father never had differences of opinion. Emily could be moulded to suit a parent's or a grandparent's will, but not so Rose, who was a natural rebel. A natural rebel and therefore closer to Faro, who had always been prepared to bravely follow the road to where his heart's desire lay.

It was dark early that afternoon. Faro was uneasy about having Rose travel from the railway station to

Newington alone, aware that she would scorn a hiring carriage and walk home, revelling in the newly fallen snow.

In view of the recent horrendous events in Coffin Lane, an area she would pass by on her way to Sheridan Place, he decided to meet the Glasgow train at Waverley Station, a few minutes' walk from the Central Office along Canongate and Jeffrey Street.

Yes, he had to see her safely home and after thinking up a plausible excuse since he didn't normally cut short his working day when there was a murder inquiry afoot, he waited eagerly for her to emerge from the crowded train.

It seemed that all of Glasgow had descended on Edinburgh and was coming to stay for Christmas with relatives or friends.

As he waited he watched the passengers hurry along the platform with the keen eye for detail that never wavered. Rose teased him that he could not even sit in a café without taking note of the other customers, what they were wearing and how that gave away so many details of their lives to the keen observer.

The unusual intrigued him. Anything out of the ordinary commanded his attention. As he told Rose, who he had trained to use her eyes and all her senses from an early age, 'There are really no ordinary people, everyone on earth is quite unique and has characteristics not shared by anyone else.'

The first woman through the barrier was lame. She wore a built-up boot and was limping along but in an obvious hurry. She was middle-aged and not very fashionably dressed, her strained anxious face suggesting that she was late for her destination; she didn't look around or expect to be met. As she seemed familiar with the area, her agitation suggested that she was late arriving or had been unable to get a seat on the earlier train, since all of them were very crowded in the few days before Christmas.

Two lovers were next, then two small children rushing forward to greet their grandfather. Then at last, as he was losing interest in watching passengers and wondering anxiously if Rose had missed the train, she emerged.

Delighted to see him she threw her arms around his neck. 'This is a great honour, Pa,' she said, laughing. 'What have I done to deserve a personal escort in the middle of your working day?'

Faro took her arm and pointed to where all the waiting carriages had swiftly been engaged. 'That's your answer. And the snow.'

Again she laughed. 'I wouldn't dream of wasting my money – you know me, Pa. I love the walk down the Pleasance in any weather.'

'Ro-se – over here.'

And there was Olivia, with Vince's coachman negotiating his way through the station precinct.

'What luck,' Olivia greeted them, as they dashed over and she opened the door. 'I had an appointment with the dressmaker and Vince remembered that you were arriving on the four o'clock train. So I decided that I'd meet you – just on the off chance. Such weather!'

She smiled at Faro. 'Great minds think alike.'

'They do indeed, my dear.' Suddenly stricken with remorse at all the work he had left on his desk at the

Central Office Faro said, 'And now I can rely on you to see Rose safely home.'

Rose looked from one to the other. 'What's all this about being seen safely home?'

Olivia shrugged. 'There's been a – well, some women attacked in Coffin Lane.'

Rose's eyes widened. 'How dreadful. Were they all right?'

Avoiding a reply, Olivia said, 'Brent – we're holding up the traffic. Jump in, Rose dear, I'll tell you all about it.'

Handing Rose into the carriage, Faro waved the two goodbye and set off back to the Central Office.

The suburb of Newington had been horrified by the three deaths. It was not the sort of thing they expected in their pleasant villas, to be close to sudden violent death. Even if they were not personally concerned, such matters threw doubts upon the respectability and desirability of their properties and reflected disastrously upon their value.

Faro sighed. There were a lot of ladies like Miss Errington in the Newington area who would feel that a mere servant's unhappy and violent end was horrifying, not so much in itself but because it might adversely affect their young daughters' chances of making successful and wealthy marriages.

To such people, maintaining a well-established position in society was of vastly more consequence than the brutal murders of three women of no importance.

Chapter Thirteen

Rose was looking forward to meeting Conan and Kate Pursley and intrigued by the idea of visiting Solomon's Tower.

'Pa tells me that the Mad Bart is quite transformed and reformed too.'

'Yes, my dear, and we are trying not to call him that any more,' said Vince. 'There's a party there on Christmas Eve. It's really for Jamie's benefit, so please try to remember that his name is Sir Hedley.'

'Idiot,' said Rose, slapping her half-brother playfully. 'Of course I will. I do know my manners, which is more than I can say for some.' She paused, frowned. 'Christmas Eve? Oh yes, I should be back in time for that.' And turning to Faro she smiled. 'I'm just here for the weekend, Pa.'

Trying to hide his disappointment he said, 'I thought you were to be home right until New Year.'

'Did I not tell you? I'm to be bridesmaid for Sally's wedding – she's a teacher at the school.'

Aware of her father's dismal expression, not concealed quite quickly enough, she patted his hand. 'But I'll be back again in time for the festivities. Promise.'

They were interrupted by the front doorbell.

Conan and Kate were ushered into the drawing room. Introductions followed.

When Rose took Conan's hand, she smiled and then frowned. 'We've met before, haven't we?'

Conan smiled. 'I don't think so.'

Rose looked across at her brother who was showing Kate a book he had recently acquired on Edinburgh's history.

For a moment she looked bewildered, then she smiled. 'It must be because I've heard so much about you.'

Conan raised an eyebrow. 'All of it good, I hope.'

'Indeed, yes,' Rose laughed.

The doorbell rang shrilly through the house.

Faro opened the drawing-room door and saw Mrs Brook speaking to Dr Spens, informing him politely that she would see if Inspector Faro was at home.

More trouble, sighed Faro as he called down, 'I'm here, Angus. Come away in.'

Angus ran lightly upstairs. 'I hope I'm not intruding. I thought I might find Dr Pursley.'

'We are about to have dinner. Perhaps you would care to join us if you haven't a more important engagement this evening?' he added, aware that neither Vince nor Conan would welcome this invitation that politeness demanded.

'I would be delighted, sir.'

Returning from advising Mrs Brook to set another place, he observed Angus bowing over Rose's hand, obvious admiration glowing from his boyish face.

Mrs Brook announced dinner and Faro's attitude was a mixture of annoyance and amusement as they trooped into the dining room and the young doctor moved swiftly into the chair next to Rose.

There he proceeded to monopolise her attention with talk about himself, his background, his father, his ambitions. Angling any conversation which threatened to remove Rose's attention away from himself, while keeping a firm and steady eye on the food set in front of him, whatever important information the visit had occasioned was apparently forgotten.

Mrs Brook had excelled herself. As ever when Rose was in residence, the meal was of mammoth proportions, including all the special dishes that her favourite lass had enjoyed in childhood days.

When at last the empty plates and dishes were removed and the diners returned to the drawing-room, all having expressed the certainty that they could not eat another bite and were incapable of rising from the table, Rose recovered enough to be persuaded to sing while Olivia played the piano, Angus not to be outdone accompanying Rose's ballads.

The applause was genuine. Whatever his failings Angus possessed an exceedingly pleasant baritone voice.

Carriages were called for and as goodbyes were being said, Faro heard Angus inviting Rose to lunch with him on his afternoon off.

She was smiling regretfully, not at all displeased.

'Where does your friend live in Glasgow?' Faro overheard Angus asking her.

'Just two streets away from my lodgings. In Briary Road. Do you know it?'

'I do indeed. What a coincidence— '

Faro turned away. He could see that even if there were no coincidence, Angus would make it his business to invent one.

But for himself the information was important.

Briary Road was where the murdered woman, Mrs Simms, had lived.

As they closed the door on their guests and returned upstairs, Rose said, 'What a splendid couple the Pursleys are. A definite asset to your little group.'

'You could almost say our family,' said Vince, 'for that is how Olivia and I regard them.'

Rose laughed. 'Now I remember. I have seen Conan before. In the station at Glasgow – Sally advised me to book a seat at this time of year and I saw him talking to one of her neighbours. What a coincidence.'

'Not really,' said Olivia. 'Conan visits his parents almost every week.'

'It's a funny thing,' Rose frowned. 'I thought for a moment that he was you, Vince.'

Olivia looked at her. 'I don't think they are a bit alike, except,' she added after a studied glance, 'except in height and they are certainly similar in build. And both have fair hair. But so has Kate.'

'In fact you could all be related,' said Rose.

'Typical Scots type,' said Faro.

'We all know Rose's weakness for seeing resemblances to perfect strangers,' said Vince. 'And she believes that married couples begin to look like each other after a year or two.'

'And their pets too,' said Olivia teasingly.

'Remember how you pointed out a striking likeness between poor old Mrs Dayley and her horrid poodle.'

'She was delighted. Quite flattered,' Rose protested.

'Wait until you meet Nero – the Pursleys' dog. That will tax even your imagination,' said Vince with a chuckle.

A shrill cry shattered their laughter at Rose's expense.

'That'll be Jamie. He's out of his bed again. He is naughty,' said Olivia wearily. 'And it always happens on nanny's night off. Or when we have company. He enjoys making an entrance – just like his father,' she added, laughingly avoiding Vince's playful slap.

'I must tell you about the charity performance the golf club is arranging, Rose. Your brother is very enthusiastic, just longing for a chance to tread the boards. We're doing *Cinderella*.'

'What fun! Will there be a part for me? Tell me more,' said Rose.

Overhead the cries became more insistent and Vince put a hand on his wife's shoulder. 'You stay, my dear. I'll have a stern word with the young fellow.'

Olivia relaxed gratefully. 'Bad timing from Jamie. If this had happened earlier Kate would have been in her element. She adores Jamie, loves any chance to cuddle and cosset him. They spoil him with toys too; a typical childless couple who would have made wonderful parents.'

'Have they been married long?' asked Rose.

'Oh, years and years. There have been several miscarriages and now – nothing. So sad.' Olivia cocked an ear towards the door and yawned. 'I think I'll retire.' Leaning over she kissed Rose and Faro. 'Our young fellow is up and about by six. I hope he doesn't disturb you too much.'

Alone with her father, Rose said, 'That's a very dynamic young man they've brought into the practice. Attractive too, in his way. I imagine Angus Spens will go far.'

'So his father believes.'

'Your new superintendent? What a coincidence.'

She was smiling and Faro asked, 'Angus seemed to find you fascinating, lass. Mutual, was it?'

'I'll tell you when next we meet, when I have that lunch with him,' she said with a teasing glance.

There was a small silence before Faro said, 'What news of Danny?'

She laughed. 'I thought you'd never ask, Pa. Remember when it was a forbidden subject with us? I'm so glad all that is behind us now and that you approve of my future husband,' she added, emphasising the word so proudly that Faro realised he need have no fears regarding young Dr Spens as far as Rose was concerned.

'But Danny's the same as ever,' she continued with a sigh. 'Everything has to be perfect, tied up serene and secure before he comes for me.'

Faro was silent.

'What about you, Pa? Are you thinking of retiring soon, now that you've completed your thirty years on the force?'

Faro shrugged. 'I'm trying not to think about it, lass. I have no intentions of retiring; perhaps a change of scene someday, that's all. I might go to America.'

Rose's eyes widened at that. 'We might go together,

begin a new life with Danny. Wouldn't that be wonderful?'

'I was only joking, lass. I've been long enough with Vince and Olivia, I certainly wouldn't inflict myself on another pair of newly-weds in my old age.'

She took his hand. 'You mustn't think of it like that. Besides, you'll never be old, Pa. Sometimes you don't seem any older than Vince – or me. And you have many rich, full years ahead of you.' With a sly glance she went on, 'We haven't given up hope of marrying you off some day – to some suitable woman.'

He shook his head sadly. 'Don't depend on that one, lass.'

Rose poked the dying fire thoughtfully and, keeping her tone casual, she asked, 'How is Ireland – ever hear from your lady writer?'

Faro sighed. 'Very occasionally, not enough to build hopes or dreams on. Let's not forget that Imogen Crowe is first and foremost a Fenian terrorist, with a price on her head. If she sets foot in this country they'll put her in prison. Her life would be forfeit.'

'You could go and see her, though. Have a holiday.'

He shook his head. 'False hopes and dreams, Rose love. I've had them all and that's where they're likely to remain – in the realms of fantasy,' he added with a sigh.

At her sorrowful expression, he hugged her and whispered, 'Thanks for caring, lass. Sorry I can't oblige you with a nice stepmama.'

'I just want you to be happy, Pa. I liked Imogen. I felt that she was right for you. I'd like fine to see you settled down before Danny and I take off together.'

She looked at him earnestly. 'I'd hate to have you left on the shelf.'

Faro chuckled. 'Spoken like a true mama! You'll do well in God's good time!'

When she continued to look grave, he said, 'Cheer up, I'm happy enough. I have Vince and Olivia, and wee Jamie, and we all get along famously. What more could a man ask for?'

She gave him a candid glance. 'You're too good to live your life vicariously through other folks' happiness. Has it never occurred to you that it's about time you deserved some of your own?'

When he made no comment she said, 'Maybe Imogen's waiting over there for you to do the asking. Like me waiting for Danny,' she added sadly.

Faro shook his head. 'You've got it all wrong, lass. If Imogen really wanted me, she'd not wait to be asked. She's that kind of woman, the kind you admire so much.'

'And what would your answer be?' Rose asked eagerly, with new hope in her eyes.

He wagged a finger at her, his smile enigmatic. 'Who knows? Wait and see.'

Chapter Fourteen

Suddenly Faro found his home was the centre of a hive of activity into which Rose threw herself with the characteristic enthusiasm and energy that marked the few occasions she spent with her family.

And now that family was extended. There was little Jamie, the 'young fellow', to dote on, to spoil and take for walks. There were more ambitious walks with her father on Arthur's Seat on the rare moments when their time at home coincided.

But most of all there was Olivia whose good works had extended to organising a benefit at the Pleasance Theatre for the Gentlewomen's Fund for City Orphans.

An amateur production of *Cinderella* was in preparation and members of the local golfing fraternity, including Vince and Conan and others belonging to a glee club, had been prevailed upon to provide some spirited singing. Meanwhile, behind the scenes of frantic rehearsals wives, mothers and sisters had been persuaded to sew or otherwise provide the costumes.

This was to be a pantomime with a difference, an all-male cast with the exception of Cinderella. It was billed as: 'A great amateur extravaganza with a talented conjurer, an acrobat and a profusion of the most popular of current music hall ballads.'

But even as plans were made, beyond cosy lamplit drawing rooms with Christmas trees and peaceful snowy gardens lay shadows of darkness and fear. For in that wintry gloom there was one unforgettable menace, the still missing madwoman, Conan's patient.

It was a time of terror when few of the area's female residents cared to travel without an escort. The days were short and nightfall descended at four o'clock, by which time solitary females glanced nervously over shoulders and recognised the wisdom and urgent necessity of heading for safety and home, with the key turned in the lock as speedily as possible.

Up to now, all attacks had been in the open, but one could never be sure that the Lady Killer's range might not be extended, the temptation of an unlocked door, somewhere to hide, irresistible.

This murky outer ring of uncertainty and lurking danger had become Faro's arena where he sought clues to the disappearance of a woman who could appear wraith-like from the dark, strike her victim with a kitchen knife (for so it had been concluded was the weapon involved) and then melt away into the night.

Where was she hiding or, more correctly Faro suspected, who was providing her with a refuge? In front of her lay Newington with its villas and their handsome gardens. Behind her the deserted barren stretch of volcanic rock and rough grass that were Arthur's Seat, broken only by the forbidding shape of Solomon's Tower at its base.

An unlikely place of concealment, Faro decided. Was there another explanation, an accomplice or a friend in the new villas with or without knowledge of her homicidal tendencies?

But who and where?

And staring up at the vast bulk of Arthur's Seat, a mass of treacherous rocks and fissures at present being combed over in all the hours of daylight by every available policeman, he wondered if there were some secret hiding place on the hill itself.

And Faro remembered the many legends of hidden chambers. Most folk tales were based on a grain of truth. Could there be some secret chamber inside the hill, some long-abandoned hermit's cave?

As each patrol of constables returned from a fruitless search, Faro could not shake off the feeling that all these killings were linked by one still-elusive vital clue. Find it and the reason for this whole series of crimes would be revealed.

He realised that one other mystery remained unsolved: the question of the bookseller's demise, which Conan insisted could not have been a coincidence.

'Possibly Celia was on a visit to him when she disappeared. That might have been her last sighting. The old man died of pneumonia resulting from the influenza. In his weakened state a fall would be fatal, according to the medical report,' Conan added, with a shake of his head.

'I am not convinced. I would like to know a great deal more about how he came by those bruises, supposedly the result of falling headlong down a flight of stairs,' Faro said firmly. 'What I want to know is did he sustain such injuries before he fell?'

Conan had persuaded Vince that his theory was right, and that the snuff-seller Bob had provided the vital clue: Dr Benjamin had been approached by a man 'not from these parts' determined to purchase the valuable book that was not for sale.

'Let's look at it this way,' said Vince eagerly. 'When he refused to sell, the prospective buyer decided to get possession by fair means or foul. The most logical explanation is that he disturbed the old man who got in his way and was trying to escape, and he pushed him downstairs.'

Conan rubbed his chin thoughtfully. 'That's how I see it, too. And the more I consider the circumstances the more certain I am that we are on to something. And if we could find our burglar then we would have a link with Celia.'

'You believe he is hiding her?' said Faro.

'I am certain of it,' was the firm response.

Although Faro could see no logical reason to link the theft of a valuable book with the murder of three passers-by in Coffin Lane, he was tormented by the haunting thought that perhaps Conan was right.

Dr Benjamin's death, the mysterious burglar and Lady Celia were related, especially as she had been known to visit the antiquarian bookshop and was on friendly terms with the old man.

Despite the lack of any evidence he could not shake off an intuitive feeling that there was a link between the four deaths and that the missing book about Edinburgh's secret past, whether fact or fiction, might hold a vital clue.

When he discussed his latest theory with Vince and Conan, his stepson smiled and nodded in his partner's direction. 'Don't you think it's time you told him, Stepfather, what you know about that locked room in Solomon's Tower?'

And so Faro revealed that during the investigation of an earlier case, alone in Solomon's Tower one day he had found what Sir Hedley referred to as his 'old charter room' with its door unlocked.

'It is actually an ancient vaulted chapel, dating from the days of the Templars, probably all that remains of the original structure hewn out of the volcanic rock of Arthur's Seat. Perhaps the Tower was built around it, to conceal its presence.'

Conan stared at him, entranced. 'And we thought its history was lost in the mists of time,' he said triumphantly. 'Well, well, this is something of a revelation, sir. Naturally I'll keep it to myself – and Kate, if I may tell her. She'll be glad to know that it is nothing more sinister; sometimes her mind drifts to haunted rooms in ancient towers, despite all her efforts to bring the furnishings up to date.' He smiled. 'She reads too many sensational novels, I'm afraid.'

With a shiver, he added, 'I have to admit it often feels like a house of secrets, I can tell you. I am not given to flights of imagination, but there is something odd about the place. Is it always freezing cold – even in summer?' he asked Faro.

'I can't say I've warmed to the atmosphere at any time,' Faro replied.

'That's interesting you should say so. Uncle Hedley assures us that it will be warmer once the snow melts and when spring comes. He seems impervious to the chill draughts.'

'Used to it, having lived there so long.'

'Come to terms, I suppose you mean, sir.' Conan sighed. 'If we survive to spring without taking pneumonia, we can consider ourselves fortunate. As you know, I'm on the constant lookout for a permanent home, but Kate has developed a strong affection for her old uncle, feels obliged to look after him in his declining years. She hopes that if we find a suitable house, we can persuade him to come with us.'

Faro and Vince exchanged glances. Conan was being too optimistic. Nothing, they knew, but death itself would remove Sir Hedley from Solomon's Tower.

After Conan and Vince had left for the surgery, Faro looked out of the window. There were stars bright above the heights of Arthur's Seat. Soon it would be moonrise.

The countryside and the fields beyond Newington were in the grip of a heavy frost. And he remembered Conan's words, that a full moon was the time that warders in asylums most dreaded, when wolves howled, and the world for the insane turned topsy-turvy.

'Do you think the snow will last much longer?' Rose asked anxiously. 'Will it still be here when I get back from Glasgow? I'm hoping Vince will take me skating on the loch.'

'We can't guarantee the weather, dear, although there seems little indication of any immediate thaw,' said Olivia who had arrived downstairs with an armful of outfits from which Rose might find something suitable for her friend's wedding.

'I'll only be away for a couple of days,' Rose protested, torn between the excitement of being a bridesmaid and missing the opportunities of skating with her half-brother again.

After great consultation, one of Olivia's most elegant velvet dresses was agreed upon, plus a delectable veiled bonnet.

Rose was surprised when her father looked in to say that he would travel back to Glasgow with her on the train.

'There's no need,' she protested. 'I'm quite capable— '

'This isn't for your convenience, lass, it's a routine police matter. Some people I need to talk to.'

'In Briary Road, Pa. Is that it?'

Faro looked at Rose and she laughed. 'I guessed by your preoccupied expression, something to do with one of your cases.'

Faro had no desire to discuss the gruesome details about the murdered women any further and Rose knew her father too well to ask questions.

But he was indeed preoccupied. His original plan to visit Glasgow to make his own inquiries had been forestalled by the third killing and now Mrs Simms' daughter would have been informed by Glasgow City Police of her mother's demise. Whatever her elevated station in life doubtless she would make the necessary arrangements for the funeral.

Faro was optimistic, however, that there might be valuable information forthcoming from a visit to

Briary Road. Rose having a friend in the vicinity was providential, an opportunity not to be missed.

When he told Vince and Conan his plans, Conan smiled. 'Will you do something for me, sir? It's my mother's birthday on Boxing Day. Would you be so kind as to look in with her present and tell her I won't manage my weekly visit until after Christmas – we'll hope to bring in the New Year with them.' He frowned. 'I'm not happy about leaving Kate or Vince to cope with this influenza outbreak. I don't trust Angus, he is too inexperienced.'

On the train journey Rose found her father less talkative than usual. At least their silences were companionable, she thought, and abandoning any hopes of their usual lively conversation took out the novel lent by Olivia, occasionally glancing across at Faro who stared gloomily out of the window.

At the station, they took a carriage, and after kissing her goodbye outside her lodgings he directed the coachman to Briary Road. The day was cold and wet but Glasgow had escaped the heavy snowfalls that had devastated Edinburgh.

It was a considerable relief to be able to walk freely along pavements for a change. Although he was hopeful when Mrs Simms' next-door neighbour, Mrs Kerr, turned out to be a cheerful woman eager for gossip, his hunch that he'd learn something had been wrong.

In this instance it had been yet another wasted journey, a lost day, since their conversation yielded not a single clue to why Mrs Simms should have been murdered on her visit to Edinburgh.

Mrs Kerr was shocked by her neighbour's death, which Faro put down hastily to an accident. When he mentioned the daughter her scorn was equal to that of the Musselburgh friend.

'Can't see her having much interest in her mother dead; she had little enough interest in her when she was alive. Although I dare say out of decency she'll pay to see her buried.

'Ida knew a thing or two about that second husband. He deliberately kept her at the door. Shame it was too when that baby, her only grandchild, should have brought them all closer.'

Faro realised he was hearing the not unusual story of a mother and daughter who had nothing in common but the accident of birth.

Mrs Kerr told him that Dora, the daughter, lived in one of the big houses facing the Botanic Gardens. 'Mr Milthorpe works for a chemical firm, travels a lot. Not a very inspiring choice for a second marriage,' she added with obvious satisfaction. 'Not that she needs money; she inherited the big house from her first husband. He was well off and a lot older than her. Left her everything.'

With Dora's married name, Faro found the house after a couple of tries. His ring at the bell was answered by the housekeeper whose careful scrutiny seemed to declare 'tradesman's entrance'. She said stiffly that madam was not at home.

He announced that he was a policeman and that the matter concerned Mrs Milthorpe's mother's recent death.

The housekeeper showed no emotion but merely nodded. 'Madam will wish to inform all her late mother's friends. She would appreciate the name of the person Mrs Simms was visiting – in Edinburgh,' she said, contriving to make it appear that no one could really be surprised that more people were not struck down in that lawless city.

While she sought pen and ink he took the opportunity to look around the parlour, a dull impersonal room with a complete absence of pictures on the walls or the fashion for groups of family photographs and children.

'Has Mrs Milthorpe any family?'

'There is a baby two months old.' Seeing his glance around the somewhat bare room, she added apologetically, 'The house is up for sale. They are moving abroad very soon.'

On the doorstep, Faro was delighted to see a hiring carriage approaching, just what he needed to take him to the other side of town where the Pursleys lived.

Hoping it was unoccupied he held up his hand.

'Yes, sir.' The coachman touched his hat, nodding assent, as Faro assisted his present fare, a black-clad young woman with a crying babe in arms, to descend to the pavement. He was rewarded by thanks and a harassed smile.

As he took her place inside and the carriage moved off, he looked back and saw her entering the house he had just left.

Mrs Dora Milthorpe, no doubt. He sat back. She looked a pleasant, pretty woman, not at all like the cruel, hard-hearted vixen he had been led to expect.

The Pursleys lived some two miles away in a quiet residential district. The house overlooked the park and was only slightly less imposing than the one he had just left, but a warmer welcome awaited him for although this was his first visit to Conan's home, he had met his parents several times when they had visited their son and daughter-in-law.

Mrs Pursley, staring over her husband's shoulder as the maid showed him into the drawing room, wore an expression of anxiety which swiftly changed to one of delighted welcome at Faro's cheery greeting.

Explaining that he was in Glasgow on police business and Conan had asked him to call, he handed over the small package with their son's message and apology, assuring them that the young couple were very well and sent their love.

'How is our lad coping with this influenza epidemic?' asked William Pursley anxiously. 'Has your family escaped?'

At Faro's reassurances Mrs Pursley sighed and rang the bell for tea. 'I do so worry about our dear Kate. She's so frail – she's had so many disappointments. I wish things could have been otherwise.'

The look she exchanged with her husband said they would love to have a grandson to carry on the family name. Annie had married long ago and there were two grown-up grandchildren.

'But Canada's a long way off,' William said sadly. 'Perhaps Inspector Faro would like to see their photos, Maggie,' he added enthusiastically.

Mrs Pursley needed no second invitation to produce the family album. There were the new generation of grandchildren, and turning back the pages,

Conan and Kate's wedding and a photograph of Conan and his sister as children.

They were not in the least alike, Conan as fair as his sister was dark. Annie was as plain as her brother was strikingly handsome, dark and thin, the image of her father, while her brother resembled neither of his homely parents and was obviously a throwback to some remote relative.

Faro found himself remembering how often siblings could look like strangers and strangers by blood show remarkable resemblances to one another. It was a situation he had encountered more than once. No doubt scientific theory would someday produce an answer.

Meanwhile he was no nearer to finding any answers to three murders in his own area.

Chapter Fifteen

Every available constable was out searching the area for the missing 'Lady Killer'. There were no new incidents, no further attacks, only some very frustrated policemen praying that she would be apprehended before their family Christmas plans were ruined.

'It's all right for the superintendent and for Inspector Faro,' they complained, 'they aren't trudging about poking over snowdrifts day and night, getting their feet frozen.'

Meanwhile, Rose returned from her friend Sally's wedding. Laying aside her bonnet her first question was, 'Is the loch still frozen over?'

Reassured that there was no sign of a thaw yet, she clapped her hands. 'Where's Vince?' she demanded.

Olivia smiled. 'He'll be home shortly. It's his half day. Conan and Angus take the afternoon surgery.'

Impatiently they awaited his arrival. At the sound of his footsteps in the hall, both rushed downstairs.

'Let's go immediately, while there's still some light left,' said Rose anxiously, afraid that Vince might be unwilling.

'What a splendid idea,' said her half-brother. 'Coming with us, Livvy?'

'Wouldn't miss it,' said Olivia. 'Jamie loves the ice. Skates, Rose? You can hire them at the loch.'

Rose pointed to her father. 'You too! I insist.'

'Yes,' said Vince enthusiastically. 'We can all do with some healthy exercise.'

Exercise and the possibility of breaking an ankle were the last things Faro needed.

'I'll come and watch you enjoying yourselves.'

Refusing to be cajoled into joining them on the ice, he was content to sit in the carriage at the roadside with Brent.

The coachman was not a talkative man and Faro's silence might have been mistaken for idleness and relaxation had such words existed in his vocabulary. Immediately his young ones reached the loch he took out his notebook and once again studied all the baffling facts, the inconsistencies regarding Conan's patient that were available so far.

Absorbed in his task, oblivious to the chill shadow of Arthur's Seat, the brightness of the early afternoon vanished behind heavy clouds.

Torches were lit to give illumination to the skaters, tiny figures, wraithlike in the gentle light, curving their way across the ice, like a tableau from a ballet. They laughed excitedly, their faint voices echoing back to him.

And then it happened.

The noise like gunfire. He started up, opened the door and ran towards the loch.

Another violent crack.

A scream. This time there was no mistaking the sound, or the wavering torches across the loch which dipped and fell.

The ice on the southern shore of the loch, more exposed to the sun's rays, had become treacherously thin. It had begun to melt.

Figures whirled, shouting warnings, stumbling back to the safety of the Duddingston side.

Faro ran down to the edge of the loch.

Vince. Olivia. Rose and Jamie.

There was no sign of them emerging from the panic-stricken group of skaters.

Dear God, where were they?

He called their names, stumbling on to the ice, shouting as the cracks continued ominously, growing closer.

Horrified, he watched a split, like an open wound, appear across the ice and water gush forth.

'Stepfather!'

And there they were.

Vince with Jamie close in one arm, Olivia and Rose clinging to his other arm.

'Thank God, thank God you're safe.'

A moment later he was helping them off the ice, Brent at his side. Sobbing, breathless, they were safely on the bank, Vince helping Rose and Olivia remove their skates.

But all was not over. They were safe, but the sounds echoing across the loch towards them were screams of terror.

Vince thrust Jamie into his mother's arms. 'I think someone's gone under the ice.'

As he turned to go back, Olivia seized his arm, cried, 'No – Vince, please, it's too dangerous.'

He shook his head. 'They may be injured. They'll

131

need all the help they can get.' So saying he thrust jacket and scarf into Rose's hands.

'I'll come with you, sir,' said Brent.

'Thank you, Brent, but no. You can't skate – and you're too heavy. Stay with the family. Please.'

Olivia, still protesting, watched him in horror, breathing, 'No, Vince, please, I implore you.'

And Faro knew what his stepson intended. He was an excellent swimmer. He would go under the ice if he thought it necessary to save a man's life.

'I'm coming with you, lad,' he said. 'No argument. I'm as light as you are. Give me your skates,' he demanded of Olivia.

'No, Stepfather. You can't skate.'

'Of course I damn well can skate. I don't do it for fun, that's all. Come on, Livvy, hurry.'

He wasn't very good at it: seriously out of practice, he hadn't been on the ice for years. Much as he would have once enjoyed such sport and activity, he had realised that there were enough daily hazards in pursuing criminals without uncalled-for broken limbs.

Twice he almost fell. Vince told him to go back and when he refused, Vince seized his arm. 'If you're determined to risk your neck then hang on to me.'

As they skated across to the scene of the accident, the ice beneath them continued to shudder and crack ominously.

At last Vince pushed his way through the sombre group huddled together a safe distance from where the ice had broken.

'I'm a doctor. What's happened?'

'A young lad fell in. They're trying to reach him.'

'He's gone under the ice— '

'He'll be drowned,' cried a girl. 'What can we do?'

'He's a goner, I'm afraid,' said her companion.

'Let me through,' said Vince firmly, watching a small figure a few yards ahead of them, lying on his belly, sliding across to where the raw edge of the ice spurted brown water.

'That's his brother,' said the man next to Vince.

They could hear him shouting: 'Timmy – Timmy, it's me. Hold on.'

Vince moved quickly. Lying down he began sliding across the ice, using his elbows gently to propel himself to the boy's side.

Faro couldn't stand and watch. In his mind's eye, he saw the ice like some distorted sheet of glass flipping over, carrying Vince and the boy's brother into the murky waters below.

On the terrified faces around him, he saw recrimination.

'You dared him to go,' said one girl, sobbing, hitting out at the boy who stood silently at her side. 'It's all your fault.'

The boy, a student by his appearance, looked shamefaced. 'It was all in fun. We were having a bet as to who could go farthest.'

Faro turned to them. 'A bet,' he said in disgust and anger. 'Innocent people may die because of your stupid bets.'

He moved aside from the group to get a closer view of Vince. Beside him the young girls in the party shivered and sobbed, clinging to each other, turning their backs on the students who had been escorting them and had been showing off with such disastrous consequences.

133

Faro guessed what had happened. The lads, full of bravura, desperate to impress, had been vying with each other. It was a game as old as nature itself re-enacted in every wild species God had created.

Now unsure whether to be brave and foolhardy before the girls or cowardly and circumspect, they hesitated, appalled by the implications of what was happening a few yards away.

They were very young, Faro felt with sudden pity. And most had elected to be cautious. One accidental death was enough.

It was not in his own nature to stand and watch, and unable to bear the suspense any longer, he tore off his greatcoat, and following his stepson's example, face down he edged his way across the ice alongside Vince and the boy's brother.

Vince heard him slithering over. 'Get back, Step-father. Get back.'

'No. You may need me.'

'You're a damned nuisance, and you're an extra weight. I don't want to have to drag you out too.' And to the boy's brother: 'For God's sake, can't you grab his arm and keep hold of it this time?'

His shoulder deep in the icy water, Vince held the boy to stop him from slipping over the edge.

'Timmy – Timmy. Oh damn – damn – I had him and I've lost him again,' he sobbed.

'How long's he been under?' gasped Vince.

'Minutes – God knows.'

Then regardless of his own safety, the boy thrust both arms into the water and screamed, 'Timmy, Timmy – I'm here, catch hold!'

Vince, who was bigger and stronger, said, 'Let me try, come on, move aside – I have longer arms.'

Reluctantly the boy let Vince take his place.

All around them now, the world had become a mountain of ice that thundered and echoed, that cracked and groaned; ominous sounds, indications that they would be next to be flung under the deadly waters.

Faro moved closer to Vince, near enough to grab him should the inevitable happen.

Vince's arms were hidden by the icy water. 'Timmy, can you hear me? Take hold, lad. Take hold. Wait – I've got him – I've got him.'

But the cry of triumph came too soon.

He had the lad by the hair but he could get no further purchase.

Faro leaned forward to help. They grabbed his shoulders, but one look at his face told them it was too late.

The boy's brother slithered forward eagerly, but with the extra movement and the strain of their additional weight, the ice began to roll.

And as they slipped forward together, the boy's head appeared briefly, his poor dead drowned face glimpsed for one ghastly moment, before it disappeared once more beneath the ice.

'He's dead. Drowned. Oh dear God— ' his brother sobbed.

There was nothing anyone could do now, no further hope of rescue.

They must save themselves.

Hand and arms, ropes, sticks, all were used to pull

the three rescuers to the safety of the still-frozen area of the loch.

Someone with a carriage bundled Timmy's brother inside, sobbing, still protesting, fighting them off desperately, determined to return to the broken ice, shouting that he must go back for Timmy. What would their mother say?

Olivia and Rose were waiting with Brent. Rushing forward, white-faced, they helped Vince and Faro into the carriage.

After a homeward journey of ten minutes that seemed like a lifetime, they staggered drenched and shivering up the steps to be met by a horrified Mrs Brook.

At last, wrapped in blankets before a roaring fire, with Olivia kneeling beside Vince, Rose, the practical, thrust hot drams of whisky into their shivering hands, but Faro felt as if he would never be warm again.

'God, what a nightmare,' Vince murmured.

'What will happen to that poor boy?' asked Rose.

Vince sighed. 'That poor boy was dead. I could see it in his face. We couldn't have saved him.'

'And you might both have been drowned too,' said Olivia angrily.

'They were both very brave,' Rose protested.

'Brave fools! That silly boy's determination to show off nearly had me a widow and you without a father. Let me remind you— '

'All right, all right,' said Faro. 'We did the best we could.'

At last with dry warm clothes and Mrs Brook's good hot soup inside them, since they had little appetite for her excellent steak pie, they were reasonably restored.

Conan arrived from the surgery and listened in shocked silence as the sad tale was related to him: a day's skating begun so light-heartedly that had ended in one family's tragedy and loss of a young life full of promise.

The dead student, it transpired, did not even belong to Edinburgh. Faro thought of his family, of that knock on the door, the policeman's sombre face and a Christmas that would remain with them for ever.

'When will they recover the body?' Vince asked.

The canal dredger's boat would have the grisly task of breaking the ice and using grappling irons to search for the drowned boy.

Chapter Sixteen

On the following afternoon Celia struck once more.

Faro was in his study sifting through the constables' reports on their findings on Arthur's Seat and street by street inquiries in the Newington and Pleasance area.

Vince had looked in from seeing a sick patient in Blacket Place and they were having a cup of tea when the doorbell rang shrilly through the house followed by Mrs Brook announcing, 'Yes, the inspector's upstairs with Dr Laurie— '

A moment later the door opened to admit a terrified, dishevelled Kate. The dog Nero was panting at her side and the two men were aware of Mrs Brook at her heels, protesting at the beast's dirty pawmarks on her clean floor.

'The inspector doesn't allow dogs in the house, madam.'

'This is an emergency. Let me past, please.'

Pushing Mrs Brook aside, she ran over to Faro and seized his hands. 'You must help me, please help me. I wouldn't have brought Nero, but I had to. No one could attack me when he was with me.'

Mrs Brook regarded the scene sternly, awaiting Faro's orders. 'I'm sorry, sir. I didn't realise— '

'Of course you didn't,' said Vince consolingly, and as Faro led the terrified Kate to a chair, added, 'Be so good as to bring us another pot of tea, Mrs Brook.'

Kate sat trembling, her nervous hands on Nero's head.

'She came to the Tower. This – woman – they're all looking for. She came and – looked at me – me through the window. She was trying to get in – to get at me.' Her voice rose wildly. 'Don't you see?'

It was almost impossible to get through her shocked and stammering outburst and make some sense of what she was trying to tell them.

Mrs Brook arrived with a tray, looked askance at the little group.

'A cup of tea, plenty of sugar in it for Mrs Pursley,' said Vince, and to Kate, 'Here you are, my dear. Drink it slowly,' he added in his best bedside manner.

At last the cup rattled back into its saucer while Mrs Brook took her time over closing the curtains and lighting the lamps against the darkness of four o'clock on a December afternoon.

The housekeeper had become accustomed through the years to emergencies in the inspector's household but her curiosity was aroused by Mrs Pursley's terrified appearance.

She lingered over her tasks, casting a sympathetic glance on the poor lady who seemed quite demented, and a less warm and more cautious consideration of that huge fierce dog.

Nero had settled himself on the rug in front of the fire as close as possible to his mistress, showing large yellow teeth and growling ominously at whichever of her dear gentlemen made a move in the poor lady's direction.

'That will be all, Mrs Brook. Thank you.'

Then at last they managed to get the story out of Kate.

Conan was on his afternoon calls and she had decided that as he didn't expect to be out very long, she would make some scones for his tea.

While she was gathering the ingredients and putting them on the kitchen table, she thought she heard someone try the back door.

'As you know, Conan insists that I keep it locked when he's out. I thought he had forgotten his key. Thank heaven it was locked and I didn't open it. I said, "Is that you, Conan?" but there was no answer.'

She shuddered and terror threatened to make her incoherent again. 'I decided that it must be one of the cats since Nero goes beserk at strangers and he hadn't moved or barked once.'

'Ah,' said Faro, seizing his opportunity. 'So you were alone in the house? And where was your uncle?'

She thought for a moment. 'I don't know. He'd be upstairs somewhere with his books, or whatever he does up there, I expect. He doesn't communicate very much these days,' she added in tones of disappointment. 'We hardly meet except at dinner. And he's taken to asking for trays in his room lately. He hasn't been terribly well; no appetite, you know. Conan's quite concerned about him.'

Kate took a deep breath, her hands twisting the lace handkerchief as she dabbed at her eyes. She seemed momentarily to have lost the thread of what she was telling them.

'Pray continue,' said Faro gently.

'Well, I thought I saw something moving outside. It was getting dusk, if you could call it that, since with this thaw setting in and so much drizzle there hasn't been much daylight to speak of. As I was looking out of the window. . .' She paused and her eyes widened in horror. Closing them, she whispered, 'A woman – looked in – she was wearing one of these old-fashioned poke bonnets; you know, the kind that milkmaids wear.'

She leaped up from her chair. 'And I knew it was – her. I've always guessed that she wants Conan – she idolises him – I knew then that she'd come to kill me. I didn't know what to do. I panicked, I had to get away, out of the tower. So I unlocked the door, just ran out – Nero followed me. And we've run every inch of the way here.' She sank back in her chair, eyes tightly closed, her face pale and exhausted.

Giving her a moment to recover, Faro asked, 'Can you tell us a little more about this woman?'

'No. No. Nothing. It was too dark to see her face – it was hidden by the bonnet. But it was awful, awful.' She sobbed anew. 'I want Conan,' she wailed.

Vince stood up. 'I'll take you back in the carriage.'

'No, no. I never want to go back there. Never.'

Vince and Faro exchanged glances. 'Very well, stay here. I'll bring Conan. And you can stay here as long as you like – Mrs Brook will prepare a bed for you both,' he added soothingly.

Leaning across he patted her arm, to be rewarded by a show of teeth and a warning growl from the dog.

'That's all right, old chap. You look after your mistress,' he said calmly.

'I'm coming with you,' said Faro, ringing for the housekeeper. He added, 'Olivia and Rose are out somewhere with Jamie, but Mrs Brook will stay with you until we return with Conan.'

Vince's carriage was at the door. Both men leaped in with one thought: that Celia might still be in the vicinity of the Tower.

That was their first priority, Conan could wait.

'There he is,' said Faro.

He was hurrying towards them on foot from the direction of the Tower, walking at a fast pace.

'Vince – thank God. I've lost Kate.'

'No you haven't, old man. She's safe with us at Sheridan Place. Get inside.'

Conan took the seat opposite and gasped, 'Safe? What do you mean safe? I came home for my tea as usual, found the door wide open and Uncle Hedley wandering about the garden. He was in a frightful state. He'd heard her screaming and come downstairs; he thought she'd been carried off. You know what he's like.'

'We're heading back, Brent,' shouted Vince to the coachman. 'If you can find a suitable place to turn us round, that is.'

'Very well, sir.'

The already narrow road, still hampered by snow-drifts, was difficult to negotiate and they had almost reached the lochside before it widened again.

'What on earth has been happening?' Conan demanded.

As Vince related Kate's terrifying experience of the woman at the window, Conan gave a horrified gasp.

142

'Celia! Dear God. That explains it.'

'Are you sure?'

'Of course I'm sure. How else would you explain what I found pushed under the back door? Kate obviously hadn't noticed it – thank God.'

And from his pocket he took a scrap of paper, torn from the top of *The Scotsman*.

'Look at this, sir.' He handed it to Faro. There were only four words, scribbled in block capitals and heavily underlined:

YOU SLUT ARE NEXT

'Celia's out to get Kate,' said Conan. 'I think I've always feared that. She wants me and in her tortured mind she has to get rid of my wife. Don't you see, her madness has taken off in another direction. Jealousy, the kind of insane obsession that a woman who loves a man to distraction would kill for.'

He seized Vince's arm as the carriage swerved dangerously and, righting itself, settled for the journey back to Newington.

'Stop, if you please, Brent,' said Faro.

'What is it, Stepfather? What's wrong?'

'I think I'll seize the opportunity of a word with Sir Hedley.' And stepping down from the carriage, he looked back at the two men. 'Then perhaps I might be able to tell you what's wrong.'

'You think – he might know something about Celia?'

'That is precisely what I am hoping. No, don't wait for me – I'll walk back.'

*

Sir Hedley opened the front door to him.

'Saw you coming. Trouble, is there?'

As he led the way along the corridor and into the kitchen, Faro noted that although he looked considerably cleaner, he was looking frailer, older. He had a particularly nasty cough and apologised to Faro.

'Can't get rid of it. Young Conan gives me some of his damned medicine, but doesn't seem to help. Doctors – never had any patience with the breed. What's happened to my niece? Rushed out as if all the devils from hell were at her heels.'

Patiently Faro explained what Kate had told them.

'This madwoman, you say. Never seen her.'

'She's known to be violent, sir. And in this vicinity.'

The old man started to speak and that resulted in another bout of coughing. 'Damn it,' he said, taking out a handkerchief. 'Damn it. Going to say I've seen all your constables searching about the hill – and in my garden,' he added with a furious glare at Faro.

'I don't suppose any of them suggested searching the Tower,' Faro said.

Sir Hedley grinned savagely. 'I'd have given them short shrift if they had,' he said grimly. 'Keep a shotgun handy for that sort of thing. They're all scared of me, anyway, don't you know. They think I'm mad – I could teach most of those young bucks a thing or two— '

Faro cleared his throat apologetically. 'But you can trust me, sir, can't you?'

''Course I can – you and your young lad. Best friends I ever had till m'niece came along. 'Course I trust you – no question. Ask away.'

'Well, sir, it's like this. This woman we're looking for, she might possibly be hiding in the Tower— '

Sir Hedley stared at him, and then laughed. 'In here – in my house, you mean?'

'That is a possibility.'

'Hiding here, without young Conan and m'niece knowing.' Again he laughed. 'Well, sir, if that's what you believe, I can only suggest you take a look around youself. Go on.'

'Thank you, sir, I was hoping you'd say that.'

Faro's search did not take long. The few rooms downstairs were neat and orderly, the cellars cold and dark, but with no evidence of anyone taking refuge there.

He doubted if there were any secret panels or apertures since the entire building was made of stone.

He searched the upper floor: Sir Hedley's bedroom, with five cats happily resting on his ancient four-poster bed. They gave him reproachful looks, a few plaintive miaows and then settled down again.

A large table, a comfortable decrepit chair and a large bookcase, with its contents tumbling everywhere, had all escaped Kate's rigorous onslaught of order and cleanliness.

There remained the strictly forbidden 'old charter room'.

Faro hesitated, then salved his conscience with Sir Hedley's permission to search everywhere.

He tried the door. To his surprise it was unlocked.

The ancient chapel was as he remembered it. He walked round carefully but there was no hiding place visible to a casual but determined searcher.

Across the corridor was Conan's study or laboratory,

as he called it, with its test tubes and lingering smell of mice, noxious chemicals, and scuttling rats. He had no desire to linger. Satisfied that the Tower was not concealing Celia he returned downstairs.

Sir Hedley greeted him triumphantly. 'Could have saved you all that. Should have believed me.' He tapped the letter he was reading. 'Young Conan is writing to the Society of Antiquaries about Kate's brooch – you know, the owl moons clasper, as they call it. After his father found that stone outside, they think there's a connection with the Tower. She meant to post it. Here, read it. You like this sort of thing,' he added, thrusting it towards Faro.

Politely skimming the contents of the letter, Faro promised to give it to Conan, pushed it into his pocket and began what now seemed a long walk back to Sheridan Place.

He took the short cut through Coffin Lane quite fearlessly. He was quite sure from some interesting fragments of information he had picked up in the last few hours that he at least was quite safe from the attentions of the 'Lady Killer'.

Chapter Seventeen

Calm reigned over Sheridan Place once more.

Conan had persuaded Kate to return to the Tower that evening.

Vince was clearly worried.

'Although he said not one word to indicate such a thing, or reveal his own misgivings, he behaved as if the whole incident was a figment of Kate's imagination. I know him well, Stepfather, I know what I'm talking about. He didn't believe a word of her story.'

Faro looked thoughtful. 'Are you suggesting that Kate is having some kind of breakdown?'

Vince nodded. 'That is a possibility.'

Both men were silent. They were fond of Kate, and Conan's reaction alarmed them with its implications.

It rained heavily that night. The snow was shifting at last. The tragedy on Duddingston Loch was reason enough to be thankful that the ice was melting and that no more lives would be lost in fatal accidents.

The thaw set in faster than anyone had anticipated and although this was a cause of lamentation for folk who believed in the romance of a white

Christmas as portrayed in sentimental paintings, the inconvenience was considerable and most of Edinburgh heaved a great sigh of relief, in particular those like Faro and other citizens who lived on the south side of the town. They had been faced with miserable journeys to work each day, forced to go on foot into the city centre since the horse-drawn omnibus notices read: 'Services withdrawn until road conditions improve.'

As for hiring carriages, they had disappeared from the Newington area since the murders. Wise cabmen were either taking elaborate precautions to neither fall victim to a madwoman on the rampage nor invite influenza by sitting in a piercing wind awaiting a fare.

In practical matters, now that the ice had broken into floats it made the dredgermen's job of recovering the student's body easier and they were out with grappling irons at daybreak.

From the safety of the lochside their activities were watched by a group of onlookers whose curiosity was sufficient to bring them shivering from warm beds on a Sunday morning.

Faro and Vince were not among the watchers. They had both seen more than enough dead bodies to satisfy even the most ghoulishly inclined. Their first indication that the boy's body had been recovered was when a constable arrived at the door to alert them and request their presence.

Reaching the loch, they had to clear a passage among the spectators to where the victim's anxious friends were waiting.

Yes, they had identified him, weeping as they did

so. His father had been summoned from the friends' house where he had awaited this melancholy event.

Even as Faro and Vince reached the group of mourners the boy's father was drying his eyes and, his voice a broken whisper, was making halting arrangements to have his son taken home.

It was a heart-wrenching moment. Faro and Vince offered their condolences but the glazed look, the shake of the man's head, said it was doubtful indeed whether he saw or heard them.

He had eyes only on the still figure of his son, lying dead at his feet, taking into oblivion all the proud hopes and dreams, destroyed in a moment's tragic accident.

A hand touched Faro's arm. 'Would you come this way, Inspector?'

Following the constable away from the sad-eyed group, he walked over to another group huddled over what looked like a large bundle of clothes by the lochside.

'Have a look at this, sir,' the constable whispered excitedly.

Faro stooped down and saw a dead face, plastered with dark hair staring up at him. Thin white hands.

The corpse was that of a drowned woman.

'We've just pulled the poor creature ashore; she came away in the grappling irons, floated towards us,' said the dredgerman. 'Must have got dislodged from the reeds when we were poking about with the rods for the lad.'

'Where was she?'

'Same place as him. Far side of the loch.'

Vince came over. 'What have we here? I'm a doctor.'

The man looked at him. 'Too late for that, sir.'

As Vince knelt down, the man continued, 'We thought we saw hair, long human hair. Grabbed it, and there she was, sir.'

Vince looked up at them questioningly.

'Doubt you'll be much good to her now, sir,' said the dredgerman. 'Dare say she made sure of that when she jumped in.'

'A suicide, you mean?'

The man shook his head sagely. 'That's right. Mark my words, sir. There were two heavy stones, roped together round her ankles. She was making sure she wouldn't be rescued, this poor lass. Probably slipped across on the ice and where it was thinnest, she just plunged in.'

'Where are the stones?' Faro demanded.

'Back in the water, sir. They came off as we were trying to disentangle her from the reeds.'

'Seems daft, doesn't it?' said his companion. 'She didn't reckon the ice-cold water was enough to kill her in seconds, poor silly woman.'

'Aye,' said the first man, 'and she might have lain there till kingdom come, till the body rotted away, right over there close to the railway line.' Again he pointed. 'No more that a few yards from where the lad fell in. She chose a fine quiet grave; not much comes and goes there in normal times, nothing but the reeds for the swans and the geese to roost in.'

'That's right,' nodded his partner. 'Could have lain there and never been found.'

'Till she rotted,' repeated the first man.

Vince was examining the woman's face and neck. Her skin was a ghastly grey.

Who was she? Faro envisaged another search through the list of missing persons, another sad family to inform. He had scant experience in such matters, but she looked as if she had been in the water for several days.

Among the morbid bystanders diverted from the departure of the drowned boy and his mourners heads rose, turning curiously in their direction. There was swift movement and excited voices alerted to the possibilities of this new tableau.

'Been another accident, has there?' someone called.

Vince hastily covered the woman with the sacking the dredgerman had produced. 'The police mortuary, I think, as soon as possible.'

The first dredgerman, a big burly chap, effort-lessly threw the now shrouded body over his shoulder and bounded smartly up the bank towards the road, followed closely by Vince and Faro.

'If only we had those two stones.'

'What on earth good would they do?' asked Vince.

'Evidence,' was the reply.

'Seems a fairly obvious suicide, I'd say,' panted Vince as they hurried after the dredgerman and his burden, ignoring the questions from the crowd who ran eagerly alongside.

'Another goner?' one persistent onlooker demanded.

By a stroke of fortune, the police carriage was still there. Summoned for the drowned boy, it had not been used since the bereaved parent had made his own arrangements and was to travel back to Glasgow with his son's body.

With the woman's corpse hoisted on to one of the stretchers, Faro and Vince took their seats alongside.

'A suicide?' asked the constable.

'We don't know that for sure,' said Faro, aware of Vince's disbelieving shake of the head.

As they drove past Solomon's Tower, Conan was walking back down the hill after taking the dog Nero for his daily exercise.

He seemed surprised to see them.

Faro leaned out. 'They've recovered another body from the loch.'

'Not another accident. God, how awful.'

'This time it's suicide,' said Vince.

'As far as we know, at the moment,' murmured Faro, who already had some new and alarming suspicions about the possible identity of the woman.

'We're taking her to the mortuary.'

'I'll come with you,' said Conan.

Thrusting Nero indoors, he called to Kate who ran out and, seeing the police carriage with Faro and Vince inside, asked, 'What's wrong?'

'Another drowning. I'm needed,' Conan shouted back to her.

As he climbed in Faro leaned over and removed the blanket covering the woman's face.

Conan gave a horrified exclamation. 'Oh dear God. No!'

'I take it you know her,' said Faro grimly.

'Know her, of course I know her. It's Celia.' He took the dead hands as if to chafe life into them again.

'Oh dear God, what a terrible thing to happen. What on earth was she doing on the ice?'

'Not on. Under,' said Faro.

'It wasn't an accident, Conan,' said Vince. 'It was suicide.'

'Suicide!' breathed Conan. Bewildered, he shook his head and repeated, 'Suicide!'

Faro shrugged. 'Well, that's what it looks like. We'll know for sure once the police surgeon's had a chance to look her over.'

But Conan wasn't listening. Furiously he banged his fists together. 'If only she'd come to me, I could have helped her.'

'She was past help, Conan,' said Vince, moved by his friend's grief. 'She obviously didn't want to live any longer. Tied two mighty great stones around her ankles to make sure she went to the bottom of the loch— '

'Where?' demanded Conan.

'Away at the far side near the railway line, where she was unlikely to be found – or rescued.'

Conan nodded miserably. 'I should have saved her from all this. I failed,' he added sorrowfully. 'She believed in me, trusted me, and when I was most needed, I failed her.'

'Perhaps she thought it was better than the hangman's rope,' said Vince. 'You can console yourself with that.'

'What a consolation,' was the bitter reply, and turning to Faro who looked grave and was unusually silent Conan added, 'At least the loch has given up your murderer, sir. And you've solved your crime.'

'Yes, we can all sleep easy in our beds now,

Stepfather,' added Vince. 'Wait until the newspapers get this. Relief all round. Everyone can relax and enjoy a merry Christmas without a madwoman with a knife on the rampage.' He smiled across at Faro. 'What a blessed relief. Another case closed, Stepfather.'

Chapter Eighteen

The madwoman was dead.

Within hours of the discovery the newsboys were out on the High Street. Among the crowds at Duddingston Loch there had been present one lucky young journalist, an eyewitness to the sensational recovery of the woman's corpse. The headline ran, 'Gruesome Find. Suicide of Lady Killer.'

In Newington residents sighed and went about their Christmas preparations with a feeling that a load of terror had been lifted. No longer need servants or their mistresses feel afraid walking out at twilight to post a letter down the street or to buy a pound of sugar.

The screeching maniac who had descended out of nowhere with knife upraised, slashing, cutting, felling them to the ground and vanishing wraith-like into the night, was dead. And by her own hand.

The feeling of reprieve was like the end of an epidemic. Among the greatest to sigh with relief was Kate, marked down as the next victim.

'Celia must have pushed that warning note through the door just hours before she walked into the loch,' said Conan. Faro looked at him, was about to say something but changed his mind as Conan continued. 'Thank God it's all over, although I can't help feeling compassion for that poor tortured soul.'

'I don't feel anything but gratitude that she's gone,' said Kate. 'My heart almost stopped – I nearly died of fright.'

Conan was not to be placated. 'I shall always feel a measure of guilt about what happened. If only I could have found the means to deal with her mind, just as one would heal a sick body.'

'It will be interesting to know what the post mortem reveals. Conan is expecting some disease of the brain,' said Vince to Faro after the Pursleys had left. 'He is far too soft-hearted for a doctor,' he added. 'Such a profession is not for the faint-hearted.'

He was mistaken as Conan, somewhat white-faced it was true, insisted on being present when Vince and Faro visited the mortuary.

Dr Craig greeted them cordially. There was nothing of the sombre dealer with sudden death in his cheery face fringed with a Father Christmas beard, which always took Faro by surprise until he realised that the police surgeon was an older version of Angus Spens: a doctor who didn't allow his work to prey on his mind or suffer from excesses of imagination.

Angus Spens had beaten them to it. He was already there, chattering excitedly. In his opinion this was an occasion not to be missed. Both doctors, the young inexperienced tyro and the older man who saw dead bodies every day, were a contrast to the sombre Dr Pursley who was looking askance at the police surgeon. He appeared to be rubbing his hands exuberantly, but they had merely caught him in the act of drying them after an examination.

As Craig laid the towel aside, his expression indicated that even he was a little taken back by Dr Spens' enthusiasm and relish for post-mortem examinations.

At a safe distance, watching his stepfather's disgusted expression, Vince shook his head and whispered, 'You must admit young Angus has the better temperament for doctoring, just you wait and see. He'll be a splendid physician in another ten years or so. He is still in the textbook phase and when he sees corpses he thinks of them only as material for dismemberment. He cannot somehow identify them with living people.'

'Downright callous, if you ask me,' said Faro.

Dr Craig beckoned to them. 'Well now, gentlemen. If you would step this way.'

Vince and Faro exchanged glances. If the unpleasant chemical smells had been less evident his manner might suggest they were being received into a select gentleman's outfitters in Princes Street.

As he raised the cover on one of the white-sheeted bodies, something between a gasp and a groan escaped from Conan.

Craig turned to him quickly. 'This woman was one of your patients, sir? You can identify her?'

Conan's affirmative was scarcely above a whisper.

'Come a little closer, gentlemen, if you will.'

Angus sprang to the fore. As Vince and Faro approached Craig said, 'The body you see before you is apparently that of a woman who died by drowning. I expected a suicide but the post mortem has revealed some unusual aspects.' Rubbing his chin thoughtfully, he continued: 'As you will know from your textbooks, Dr Spens' - again in the limelight, Angus beamed delightedly - 'the cause of drowning is asphyxia. In other words— ' he paused as if conducting an anatomy lecture, speaking slowly and particularly to Faro on the off chance that the Inspector might be completely ignorant of medical knowledge. 'In other words, the air is prevented from reaching the lungs, and the oxygen supply vital for survival is cut off.'

He sighed solemnly, regarding the dead woman again. 'Of course, there is "dry drowning" in which the subject dies of cardiac arrest or laryngeal spasm caused by the shock of falling suddenly into water. Icy water would be particularly responsible for this effect.'

'Which could well be the cause in her case,' said Conan. 'We are aware that she plunged into the loch— '

'Yes, yes, Dr Pursley.' The police surgeon did not like this interruption. 'But as I told you there are other aspects which do not conform to that theory. The presence of foreign matter - the cadaveric spasm - in which weeds or similar material from the water are sucked into the lungs; even suicides, alas, cannot forgo this spasm. This last fight for breath is the body's automatic reaction— '

'What are you trying to tell us?' demanded Conan.

Dr Craig looked at them. 'We have every reason to believe, since her lungs were clear of any foreign matter, that life was already extinct before she had contact with the icy water.'

'How long has she been dead?' Faro put in quickly.

'From the bleached and wrinkled condition of her

skin which you will observe, gentlemen, – see, in places it has become loose, almost detached from her body – I should say at least six days.'

'Six days,' Faro repeated thoughtfully. 'Are you sure?'

Dr Craig gave him a supercilious smile. 'As sure as my years of dealing with drowned corpses can accurately assess, Inspector. Although it would be difficult to give an exact time since the icy water might have had a slightly delaying effect on these skin changes.'

There was a horrified gasp of disbelief from Conan.

'We have evidence that she was alive yesterday,' said Faro.

The doctor frowned. 'Then I am afraid, Inspector, that your evidence is unacceptable – for once.' He added a somewhat mocking bow, acknowledging Faro's superiority in such matters.

'The state of the body is indisputable. The corpse has without a shadow of doubt been in the water for six days at least.'

The post-mortem findings could hardly be questioned and as they left Conan was visibly shaken.

Faro was also perturbed. This was not at all what he had expected. If Celia had lain in the loch for more than one day, least of all several days, how could Kate have possibly seen her at the Tower? How to account for the warning note pushed through the door?

But if the face at the kitchen window and the note could be accepted as truth, and the evidence of the post mortem was indisputable, then the case of the

Lady Killer was by no means solved. The existence of a second assassin had become a powerful possibility.

And as if interpreting his thoughts, Conan said, 'There is one explanation. Suppose Uncle Hedley wrote that note himself . . .'

'Wait a moment. You're surely not suggesting that he was trying to scare her?' asked Faro.

Conan thought for a moment, then shook his head. 'You know what he is like, eccentric, quite wild at times.'

'By wild, do you mean mad?' said Vince.

'Not at all. Not like – like– ' Conan stopped. 'His wildness is of the harmless kind; it lies more in the region of practical jokes, of springing out at people, a schoolboy's pranks. Kate's mama said he was a terror for that sort of thing, frogs in the soup, dead mice in the bed – all the nastinesses small boys get up to– '

'Conan,' said Faro patiently, 'are you trying to say that he doesn't know the difference between childish but unpleasant practical jokes and murder?'

'No, sir, of course not. I'm just trying to find a reasonable explanation,' said Conan desperately. 'The note might have lain under the doormat for several days and he had just found it.'

The explanation seemed lame indeed and he was aware of their stern glances.

'As a matter of fact he had a difference of opinion with Kate, now I remember, earlier that day. Something about his precious cats, one of them stealing a pork chop off the kitchen table and being sick all over our best bedspread. Kate smacked the little beast.

'He doesn't seem to notice such things but Kate is a stickler for cleanliness. To put it mildly she's fed up with her uncle's cats; they have precedence over humans in the house. It's one of the reasons she is anxious to find another place to live.'

There was silence for a moment then Faro said, 'Are you suggesting that he took his revenge by putting on one of her bonnets— '

'Kate doesn't possess a poke bonnet, sir. That I do know.'

'Then doubtless there was one somewhere in the Tower. So you are saying he put it on and stared in at the kitchen window to scare her, and then he pushed a note under the door,' said Vince grimly.

Conan looked thoughtful. 'We know that he was called the Mad Bart, so I suppose anything is possible. Perhaps he wants to be rid of us.'

'But I understood that he was glad to have your company.'

'At first, yes. But you cannot imagine how secretive he is. I expect it's the result of a hermit-like existence all these years. Kate is very loyal but he has been very disagreeable lately, accusing us of spying on him and going into his beastly old charter room, as he calls it. Nothing but an empty chapel, but he insists that it is out of bounds.'

Faro, who knew considerably more about Solomon's Tower and its secrets than he was prepared to discuss, decided to have another meeting with Sir Hedley. The old man liked him; perhaps he could throw some light on the events of the night Kate had arrived in such a panic.

He was convinced that Sir Hedley was a harmless eccentric, and bearing in mind his hearty dislike of children and small boys in particular, Faro marvelled that he had made an exception in the case of young Jamie Laurie. Being the son of Vince, whom he idolised, had made the lad extra special and given him special privileges.

As Faro approached the house, his earnest hope was that he might get the old man to confess that he had been playing a practical joke on his niece, just to pay her back for chastising one of his beloved cats.

Otherwise – there was a situation developing too monstrous to bear serious contemplation.

Chapter Nineteen

At Solomon's Tower, Kate opened the door to him, clad in a large apron and dusting flour off her hands.

Faro was surprised to have interrupted her obviously at work in the kitchen; most doctors' wives had servants; then he remembered that Sir Hedley had dismissed the maid for prying.

Interpreting his glance, Kate apologised and, untying her apron, led him into the now immaculate parlour with its new curtains, chair covers and the clean smell of polish.

He looked round approvingly. 'Is this all your own work, Kate?'

She sighed. 'Indeed it is. But not entirely out of choice. Uncle Hedley rates servants just one step above beggars and one below thieves. He has never had strangers in the house and tells us firmly that he is too old to start now.'

She shrugged. 'When we first arrived, I accepted it with good humour, believing that I could change his mind. True, he has relented and I can have a servant but I am to be responsible and so forth. Frankly, after the last fiasco I've decided having a maid is more trouble than it's worth until we find a permanent home.'

She paused and smiled at him. 'Is this a social call? Conan isn't here just now.'

'It was actually your uncle I wanted to see.'

'He's still abed. He hasn't been very well these last few days – or so he claims; one can never tell whether he just wants to be left undisturbed. I've been taking all his meals up to him – and I have to tell you, bringing back the tray untouched most of the time. Conan is anxious about him: he has a cough and we suspect that he may have the influenza, but he refuses to be examined, protests that it is only a sniffle.' She shook her head. 'What would you do? I am at my wit's end to know what to do next.'

'May I see him?'

'If you think it will do any good, Conan and I would both be much obliged to you.'

The answer to his tap on the bedroom door was an angry: 'What is it now? What do you want?'

When Faro answered, there was a distinct change of tone.

'Do come in, Inspector.'

And as Faro went into the darkened room, 'So glad to see you, dear fellow. Be so good as to open the curtains, will you?'

Having done so, Faro turned to face the figure in the bed. It was obvious that the old man was not at all well, although his reply to Faro's 'How are you today, sir?' was as vigorous as ever.

'Do sit down. Come for a chat, have you? Good to see you.'

After the polite preliminaries, and an enquiry after the health of young Dr Laurie and wee Jamie,

Faro realised that any enquiries about practical joking must wait.

'I gather that your niece is looking after you very well.'

Sir Hedley grunted. 'Don't need looking after. Damned nuisance they are with all their goings-on. Making a mess of my house. Changes and all that. Can't abide change. Nosy too. Always ferreting about – just like her mother.'

It was surprising to hear Sir Hedley refer to his sister since Faro could not imagine him in youth and suffered under the extraordinary delusion that he had been born into the world an old man in the same manner as Solomon's Tower had always appeared to be a part of the landscape, hewn from the volcanic rock of Arthur's Seat itself.

As he listened to the old man's tirade, he realised that Kate's original plan of living in Solomon's Tower and taking care of her uncle was not proving a success after all.

It was obvious that the old man had swiftly grown tired of having to share his house with his niece and her husband. All her well-meaning attempts to make it more comfortable had simply taken on the aspect of interfering with a way of life that he had grown accustomed to and accepted through the years, however frightful it might seem to others.

Faro recognised sympathetically that the old man had lived alone too long to reform old habits, and to be sociable with any creatures other than his cats.

Sir Hedley pointed to a paper on the desk. 'That is their latest effort,' he said grimly. 'Take a look.'

It was a drawing of the owl stone that had been

165

found in the garden, alongside a sketch of Kate's. The drawing had been copied from a very old book bound in faded leather. Faro picked it up and studied it carefully.

'That interests you, does it? Can't make head nor tail of it myself. All that old Scots writing. Can't abide it.'

'Where did it come from?'

Sir Hedley shrugged. 'Kate gave it to me. Picked it up in some old bookshop, I suppose. What d'ye think of the drawing?'

'It's very good,' said Faro politely, his mind elsewhere.

'Now they want some archaeologists' society or other to send people out here to investigate, to dig up my garden. Won't have it. Dead against that sort of business. House crawling with strangers.'

Faro was hardly aware of him as he studied the drawing and something touched a chord.

The owl moons clasper. Seeing the words written down –

He could hardly keep the excitement out of his voice as he held up the drawing. 'I wonder, sir, may I borrow this?'

'Take it, take it.'

Kate was no longer in the kitchen. He could see her at a washing line in the garden. He called to her and she answered, but when she reached the gate it was in time to see him walking rapidly in the direction of Newington.

Before he spoke to anyone, he had to be sure of his facts.

*

He found his home had been taken over. Final preparations for the forthcoming production of the pantomime for the city orphans had invaded Sheridan Place.

In the true tradition of pantomimes, most of the cast were to be male, played by members of the golf club. The exceptions were Cinderella and the Fairy Godmother, since even Vince, who masterminded the production, realised that having these two roles played by men was calculated to destroy the last vestiges of magic that might survive the performance.

As this was an amateur production using local talent, it was not quite the thing for respectable Edinburgh ladies to appear on stage and show off their legs. Indeed, professional actresses in 'breeches parts' were still regarded with suspicion by conventional folk, and regarded as just one step above street walkers.

Bearing in mind that some of his patients might be in the audience, Vince decided to play Prince Charming 'since he is off stage most of the time and can attend to other matters'.

Faro suppressed a smile, realising that his stepson had always had secret yearnings to be an actor. Now he seemed to be doing remarkably well in the role of director too.

He had persuaded Olivia to play the role of Fairy Godmother. When she expressed some doubts, he assured her that she would be respectably clad in a long gown.

Angus Spens was delighted to be offered the role of one of the Ugly Sisters, along with a quiet young lawyer recently called to the Bar whose early inclinations were to the stage rather than the law courts.

'Doubtless he'll give a superb performance in both,' said Conan. 'I can see him as a judge one day.'

He had declined a role. 'Someone must be on duty at the surgery. Patients can't be relied upon to stay well while we prance about the stage,' he added reproachfully.

The roles of Buttons and the Baron were played by fellow golfers, their female relatives and a small army of maids relegated to making costumes and, nearer the day, preparing the feast that would follow.

Who should play Cinderella?

It was choice bound by diplomacy worthy of the court of St James itself. For whoever was offered the coveted role might provoke anguish and even future ostracism by the other wives with daughters.

Vince groaned. 'It was all to be fun. Now everyone is taking it seriously. I can see bitter feuds and members resigning en masse due to family pressure,' he added gloomily.

Conan came to the rescue. 'Simple. Put all the names of those willing into the hat and select one.'

'That's the fairest way,' agreed the secretary of the golf club, relieved that his wife, who would have contemplated with horror 'making an exhibition of herself', was not included.

The main contenders were present at the draw.

'And the name of Mrs Kate Pursley came out of the hat!'

Kate refused to believe Vince.

Gallantly she offered to withdraw but Vince would not hear of it.

'You allowed Conan to put your name forward,' said Olivia.

'He didn't ask me,' was the weak reply.

'Kate was the right choice,' said Olivia afterwards. 'She has a lovely voice and she's so slim and pretty,' she added loyally.

'I just hope she's well enough for all this,' said Conan, watching her anxiously. 'She hasn't the most robust health; one tends to forget that her enthusiasms are stronger than she is.'

Plans had become more ambitious. For the children there would be a matinée followed by an evening performance for the grown-ups at the Pleasance Theatre.

Sadly, however, Conan's gloomy prediction was right.

Kate would be unable to appear. Conan reported that she had been sick all night and another Cinderella must be found at very short notice. Kate just wasn't up to it.

Olivia looked searchingly at Rose.

'No,' laughed Rose. 'Not me.'

'Yes, you,' said her sister-in-law firmly. 'After all, you've had some experience.'

'School plays, that's all.'

'That's more than Kate had. Come along, dear. You can sing and you're the right age too.'

As for Faro, regarding the scene, it seemed that Vince was obsessed by the pantomime. Normally so acute, his stepson had, along with everyone else concerned, dismissed the tragic implications of the discovery of the woman in the loch.

He sighed. He must solve this case alone, but he

had one vital clue Sir Hedley had put into his hands, the one thread leading through the labyrinth.

He was beginning to understand why the murders had been committed and had not his immediate family been involved he would have politely declined that invitation to the evening performance.

Faro was never very good with amateur productions and he had more pressing and urgent issues on his mind. But at the last moment, Kate insisted on accompanying him.

She arrived at Sheridan Place, pale and exhausted but assuring them all that she felt much better. Besides, she so wanted to see her friends on stage.

As the curtain rose, Faro was suddenly glad that he had come after all. He felt very proud of Rose, who was bewitching as Cinderella. Her appearance was greeted with tremendous applause and, certain that the audience found his daughter as captivating as he did, he felt that was worth coming for alone.

Interested in the reaction to his family and hoping for favourable comments, he found himself shamelessly eavesdropping on the women next to him.

'Buttons, well, well, looking as if butter wouldn't melt in his mouth. No one would believe he's the undertaker's assistant, my dear.'

'And the Baron there. That villainous moustache. You'd never believe he's my solicitor in real life. Well, well, he's as pompous on stage as he is off.'

The Ugly Sisters failed to make the right impression.

'Pity they couldn't have afforded real nice big hats. Those poke bonnets are so ugly.'

'It hides their hair anyway, they wouldn't need to wear wigs. I expect that's why they chose them.'

'My dear, everything has to be the cheapest possible these days.'

At his side, Faro was aware that Kate had given a hardly suppressed moan of pain. He looked at her quickly. Her eyes were closed and she was trembling.

'What is it, my dear?' he whispered. 'Are you feeling unwell again?'

Her face deathly pale, she murmured, 'No. No. I will be all right. Just a spasm.'

The acrobat had taken over the stage.

'Are you sure?' Faro said. 'Would you like me to take you out for a breath of air, until this act is over?'

'No, really, sir. Thank you.'

The Ugly Sisters returned and the two women continued to make comments mostly of an adverse nature.

'They make convincing women, all the same,' said the less acid of the pair, prepared to be charitable. 'At least they are both tall and slim and I think the poke bonnets were a good idea.'

'Shhh,' murmured someone in the row behind.

Faro was gratified that Cinderella's singing was richly applauded and there were sentimental tears at the transformation scene although it did not go quite as smoothly as they had hoped.

There were some struggles with Cinderella's coach, pulled across the stage by a mutinous donkey, and it could be seen that the hastily donned ballgown did not conceal all her rags.

The two women alongside Faro applauded loudly.

171

As they were leaving Faro heard their final pro-
nouncement on the evening's entertainment.

'It could have been better, of course.'

'Never mind, my dear. It was a good try.'

And perhaps that was the verdict of the entire
audience as the cast returned exhausted to remove
make-up and costumes and, most important, count
the takings at the box office.

Kate returned to Solomon's Tower in Vince's carriage and Newington residents walked home happily
that night, at ease and at peace with their little worlds
from which all danger had been averted.

They no longer walked in fear of a madwoman
who had escaped from an institution, committed
three murders and then drowned herself in the loch's
icy waters.

There was moonlight and a heavy frost which
would harden the surface of Duddingston Loch,
making it once again fit for skating during the festive
season.

Banishing all thoughts of recent tragedies, they
turned their attention to Christmas and Hogmanay
and bravely made good resolutions for the forthcoming year.

Faro slept badly that night. The Pleasance Theatre
had old unhappy memories for him. And now they
were returning. Old sad days, dreams and hopes that
had died on that stage.

He turned restlessly. A moon shone brightly
through the window; perhaps that was what had
awakened him for he could not abide to sleep with

the shutters tightly closed, although Mrs Brook insisted that the night air was bad for everyone and firmly closed them each night when she turned back his bed.

Moonlight.

He got up and went to the window. The house was silent.

There was something troubling him. The ghost of a woman's shrill comments that evening, something to do with the pantomime that wasn't quite right.

What was it?

Then quite suddenly, he moved in his chair, sat bolt upright. He remembered what it was now.

He saw again the final line-up of the cast. The Ugly Sisters in their absurd poke bonnets.

Was that why Kate had trembled at his side and seemed ready to faint?

Moonlight. He saw again vividly the owl moons clasper on Kate's cloak as she fell sobbing into the hall downstairs on that fatal evening when the madwoman looked in her kitchen window.

With heart beating fast, he went to his desk, turned up the lamp and wrote some words on a piece of paper. He studied them carefully, frowning, rearranging.

Then with a cry of triumph he knew he had one part of the answer. But until he had found the right place for that fragment he must at all costs remain silent, keep this vital information to himself.

Other lives were at stake, unknowingly; innocent lives.

And – he gripped the arms of his chair – he must

move with all possible speed. He had not an hour to lose if he was to prevent the final murder.

For he knew as clearly as the moonlight spreading through his bedroom, that all that had happened was but a preliminary to another crime.

Chapter Twenty

Mrs Brook was surprised to hear the front door close while she was attending to the kitchen stove and stoking the fire that morning. Staring out of the basement window, for it was still dark outside, she thought she saw the figure of Inspector Faro in his greatcoat hastening past the street lamp outside their door.

'Where on earth is he going at this early hour, and without his breakfast?' she said, grimly adding to no one in particular that she didn't know what this house was coming to these days.

Two floors above her head, Jamie awoke, and shrilly drew attention to his regular morning requirements while Nanny Kay and Olivia's personal maid Mary left their beds sleepily, shivering in the chill dawn air.

By the time the rich aroma of bacon, eggs and sausage frying had penetrated the upper layers of the house and had lured Vince and Olivia into the dining room, it was evident that the inspector would not be returning to breakfast with them, his habit since Jamie's birth and the removal of the surgery into separate premises.

'The inspector left a note on the hall table, Mrs Brook,' said Vince. 'Yes, I expect he'll be back tonight.

No, I can't say whether he will be with us for supper,' he added a trifle sharply. 'We shall have to wait and see.'

He found the housekeeper easily upset these days by the slightest alteration in her ritual of meal times, a condition he and his stepfather were frequently unable to fulfil. Even before his marriage it had been a daunting task.

Mrs Brook was not pleased at such lack of precision, especially as Mrs Laurie was also indifferent to meals served on time since she was frequently engaged with Mrs Pursley in good works, while excellent cooking went to waste.

Miss Rose understood that Food and Cleanliness were only one step removed from God as far as Mrs Brook was concerned. She listened patiently to the housekeeper's complaints that she was not being unreasonable in needing information well in advance if any members of the family were to be absent.

'Papa frequently has tasks that require urgent attention – to do with the police, you know,' she reminded the housekeeper gently.

Mrs Brook beamed on her. Here was a lass who would go far, she thought, watching her contentedly taking second helpings of everything as the front door slammed on Dr Laurie.

At the surgery the two doctors were already confronted by a long line of patients shivering in the waiting-room, the later arrivals looking enviously at the coveted chairs already occupied near the fire.

Conan poked his head out of the surgery. 'Angus

is late – as usual. He should have been here an hour ago. I don't know what he thinks he's at,' he grumbled.

One glance told Vince that they had a serious situation. Most of the patients were exhibiting the effects of influenza and coughs.

'As is my poor wife,' Conan muttered to Vince as they met in the surgery's dispensary later. 'I left her in bed this morning. She is far from well. She was very upset, had promised to see Olivia – about this damned pantomime business.'

Conan's forebodings were right. Kate failed to arrive for a working lunch at Sheridan Place and a discussion regarding the profits accruing to the orphans. As with all such ventures there was an unforeseen and alarming list of bills to be settled first.

'I warned her she wouldn't be fit enough to leave the house,' said Conan that afternoon. 'She really does take on far too many engagements. We – or rather she – forgets how delicate she is. I should have forbidden her to get involved with the pantomime. But she gets so much joy out of helping others and refuses to regard herself as an invalid,' he added forlornly. 'This heart condition – it's getting steadily worse, I'm afraid.'

Both doctors knew the serious nature of Kate's illness.

'At least as her doctor you can look after her properly; that is the best possible treatment,' said Vince.

'I know all that, old chap. But as far as Kate is concerned I am still only her husband and she refuses to take me seriously. I've asked her to let you give a second opinion. Maybe she'll take your advice,' he said as they put on their coats to leave the surgery.

'I'll do it gladly.'

Conan shook his head. 'Be prepared for the same response as I get. She'll insist that we're making a great fuss and that she's as strong as a horse. She says that I cosset her too much and that if we'd had children, I would have had more important things to worry about.' He sighed bleakly. 'She adores wee Jamie. It has meant so much to her having Olivia as a friend.'

'Poor Kate,' said Vince. 'I know how terrible it was for her losing those early pregnancies.'

'And for me, don't forget,' said Conan bitterly. 'It is terrible for a man never to prove his manhood. Never to have a son.'

'It could be fatal now if she had a child,' said Vince.

'I know. I know. And I leave it to your imagination what the prospects of the rest of our married life are like, always haunted by fear of another doomed pregnancy.'

Vince's carriage was waiting to take Conan back to Solomon's Tower. 'I'll give her your regards – and your advice, old chap.'

'Do, please. Tell her how concerned we are about her.'

'I will. If this is the onset of influenza, perhaps if we get it in the early stage she'll be better in a few days.'

'Try out our new cough medicine,' said Vince. 'It's worked well on some of the patients. Brought down their fevers, at least.'

Conan closed the carriage door. 'Knowing Kate, she'll not want to take anything; let nature take its course, she'll say. Women are impossible sometimes,' he added despairingly.

'They're certainly more stoic than we are,' said his friend. 'Nature made them that way, I suppose, having so many more pains to bear.'

Chapter Twenty-One

Faro returned from Glasgow late that evening, hoping to talk to Vince. But he and Olivia had seats for the theatre and Rose was with them. Mrs Brook, somewhat tight-lipped, told him that her dinner was not required. They were to dine at the Café Royal and would not be home before midnight.

'Never mind,' said Faro. 'I could eat a horse. I haven't eaten all day.'

Mrs Brook was placated and gratified, although the inspector's attention to her steak pie and rhubarb tart was less complimentary than usual. He ate hungrily but was very involved with his thoughts, a deep frown creasing his forehead, and he sighed deeply and shook his head with considerable force from time to time.

It was midnight when the trio returned.

Vince had obviously dined and in particular wined exceedingly well.

'I must get him up to bed,' whispered Olivia as Vince staggered across the room and sank into a chair, closing his eyes firmly. 'Don't fall asleep there, darling.'

Rose yawned. 'Me, too. I'm so sleepy.'

Seeing her father's grim expression as he looked

at Vince, she added apologetically, 'We all needed some cheering up after an evening of Ibsen. Goodnight, Pa.' She gave him a goodnight kiss and at the door she turned. 'Guess who we met in the interval at the theatre?'

'Angus Spens, perhaps,' said Faro grimly.

Her eyes widened. 'How did you guess? You must be psychic!'

'Not at all. You looked so pleased— '

'Pleased! We couldn't get rid of him. Thought he was coming to the Café Royal with us. He practically begged for an invitation.'

'How did you get out of that?'

She kissed his cheek gently. 'By diplomacy, the way you brought me up, Pa. I promised to lunch with him – alone,' she added with a teasing glance.

Olivia was watching Vince. 'Give me a hand to get him upstairs, will you, please?' she said to Faro.

They got him into bed while he muttered protests about being fine and giggled rather a lot.

Faro gave one last unhappy look at his already snoring stepson. What a time to choose for this bout of happy inebriation when all his senses were most needed.

Closing their bedroom door, he had never felt in such utter despair, in such urgent need of confiding in Vince the dire evidence he had accumulated that day.

There was no one he could turn to and although he got undressed and went to bed, knowing nothing more could be accomplished that night, he realised he would sleep little, for he had in front of him a sad and monstrous duty.

Inspector Faro was deeply troubled. Mrs Brook observed that he had left the lamps burning. He was a stickler for safety in the home and he was not usually so absent-minded.

And Mrs Brook was right.

By four o'clock Faro had turned over every eventuality in his mind. He had gone over the evidence piece by piece, praying that somewhere he had taken a wrong turning, made a grievous mistake.

At last, knowing that sleep was impossible and he was to need all his wits about him for the task ahead, he decided to take some of the doctors' 'Soothing Elixir for Restful Slumber'.

The result was disastrous. Exhausted by the previous day's events he slept for nine hours and awoke feeling drugged and dazed.

He dressed and dashed downstairs to be met by Rose in the hall donning her bonnet.

'Had a good night's rest, Pa? I'm rushing off to meet Livvy.'

'For God's sake, Rose, why didn't someone wake me?'

Rose looked surprised. 'Was it so important?'

'Of course it was important. I always get up at seven.'

Rose sighed. 'I'm to blame, Pa. I thought you were looking so tired last night I told the others that you were needing to sleep on, the way you've been missing meals. Vince and Livvy agreed – Pa!'

But he was already out of the front door rushing along the street. At least the cold air alerted his senses again but as he arrived at Vince's surgery, he noticed that the carriage was not parked in its usual place.

His fears were confirmed when a notice on the door read: 'Doctors visiting patients. Please put urgent messages in box provided.'

He scribbled a note adding: 'Come at once. This is a matter of life and death.'

On the off chance Vince might look into Sheridan Place, he returned home where Mrs Brook was to report later that the inspector ran into the house in a great state, as she put it, demanding to know where Miss Rose was meeting Mrs Laurie.

When she said: 'I overheard them discussing Princes Street,' he swore, which wasn't like him, and asked if Jamie was out with Nanny Kay.

'No, Inspector. This is her afternoon off. Dr Pursley looked in earlier and I heard him offering to take Jamie off their hands for the afternoon as he hates going to the shops.'

'And no, Inspector,' she added. 'I didn't see them leave. It must have been while we were in the laundry room ironing.'

Faro hardly listened.

On the main road there was not a hiring carriage to be seen.

He no longer had time to waste searching for one and he trotted briskly in the direction of Solomon's Tower.

He did not ring the bell this time but quietly let himself in at the back door, which was unlocked.

So there was someone at home after all. Listening carefully he thought he heard a voice from upstairs.

Walking soundlessly up the stone spiral, he tapped

gently on the door of Kate's room. There was no answer and glancing inside, he saw that she was in bed apparently sleeping.

Sir Hedley was dozing in a chair by the fire.

He left them and ran upstairs to the Templars' Chapel, silent, sinister in the dim late-afternoon light with its ancient cross on the wall above the stone altar.

As he was examining it, a sound alerted him.

Carpet-slippered, soundlessly, Sir Hedley appeared at the door, clutching an ancient pistol which Faro did not doubt by his grim expression was loaded and which the old man with provocation would not hesitate to use.

'So it's you, Faro. Thought we had an intruder. Went in to see m'niece, must have fallen asleep. You've no right to be in here, sir. Strictly private. Have strict instructions about that, y'know. None of anybody's business but my own. Sacred trust and all that sort of thing.' He pointed to the cross. 'What are you about, sir?' he demanded.

'The owl moons clasper, sir, that's what I am about. It's an anagram of Solomon's Tower Chapel.'

Sir Hedley laughed. 'So you solved our riddle.'

'You've always known?'

'Of course. And that old book Kate lent me. That would have helped. But those two were after the wrong thing. Could have saved them the trouble of searching.'

From his pocket, he took an ancient key which he inserted in the rose centre of the cross. It sprang open to reveal a stone niche in the wall.

'See it? Held the sacrament once, perhaps even

that mysterious treasure the Templars brought with them from Jerusalem. Their holy grail – maybe. Who knows? No one has ever solved that particular riddle, have they? The treasure, that damned French gold, whatever it was that all the fuss was about – went long since. If it ever existed, which I doubt.'

He nodded towards the empty niche. 'Always been empty in my time, nothing but a piece of old wood inside. Didn't want to throw it away— '

'Where is it now?'

He shrugged. 'Your wee lad was playing with it on my desk. Said he could take it away with him— '

'If only you had told the Pursleys, sir.' How could he begin to explain the dreadful truth? 'People have died— '

The old man stared at him and grinned. 'People have always died, innocent and guilty alike, where money is concerned.'

Another voice came from behind them. 'And it isn't over yet, I'm afraid.'

Conan stood framed in the doorway, with Jamie in his arms. 'I'm sorry to inform you both that Kate is dead.'

Chapter Twenty-Two

'Kate has just died,' Conan repeated in a voice devoid of all emotion.

Sir Hedley gave a shout of disbelief and ran towards the door. 'Let me go to her, let me go to her.'

Conan stood aside. 'As you please.'

They heard him shuffling along the corridor as Conan turned to Faro and, still carrying Jamie, indicated a chair. 'We might as well be comfortable for a while.'

'Let me take him.'

'No, no, you'll wake him.'

Faro looked at Conan with the sleeping child in his arms, trying to reconcile what he saw and what he had believed of this man's essential goodness, his dedication to saving lives, with this terrible reality, this gross betrayal.

'You killed Kate, didn't you?'

Even as he uttered the words he hoped for a passionate denial or for some shattering rational explanation which he had overlooked in the evidence that pointed so steadily at Conan.

'Of course I didn't kill her.' Conan shrugged. 'She was dying; we all knew that.' But as he spoke he avoided Faro's eyes and there was a sense of triumph he was unable to hide, of matters that had gone according to plan.

'For God's sake, why did you hate her? What had she ever done to you?' Faro demanded.

'I didn't hate her. That's too strong a word. Indifferent, yes, I have been indifferent for years.' He paused and looked down tenderly at Jamie. 'I suppose it began when I knew there would never be a live child.'

Faro regarded him steadily. 'It was always Kate, wasn't it?'

'I don't take your meaning.'

'Kate was always the intended victim. You wanted rid of her so you killed the others to make it look as if your patient Lady Celia was responsible.'

'That's a preposterous suggestion. Are you out of your mind? Celia killed them all.'

Faro's face was expressionless and with a sigh of exasperation Conan said, 'I'll tell you what I know of the first murder. She went that afternoon to call on Dr Ben in his bookshop, as she so often did. Well, she found him dead. She thought someone had killed him and that she'd be blamed. That threw her back over the edge. She heard someone at the door, ran into the kitchen, picked up a knife to defend herself. Panicked and ran for her life.'

He shook his head. 'She needed me desperately. I was the only one who could help her. She was madly in love with me – I think you probably guessed that. I still don't know, and we never will, why she killed that maid Molly. Perhaps she was lost, asking the way to Solomon's Tower and the maid got in her way . . .'

As Conan spoke, suddenly Faro could see it all

187

happening. The maid rushing out of the house into the night after a bitter quarrel with her mistress. Distraught, running away – and running towards Celia, also distraught. But with a knife in her hand.

In that last moment did she believe that Molly had been sent to pursue her, take her back to the asylum?

'And when she did reach you,' Faro said, 'and you knew she had killed Molly, you realised you couldn't help her any more. She'd be locked away for the rest of her life. Was that when you got the idea? Why not make it worthwhile. Another couple of murders she'd be blamed for. And then Kate— '

'They weren't meant— ' Conan bit back the words.

'To die.' Faro completed for him grimly. 'But die they did. First of all, however, you had to get rid of Celia.'

'It wasn't like that at all. I never intended to harm her. I even tried to persuade her to go back to the asylum with me, give herself up. She turned violent at that – hitting out at me. Madness and fear gave her terrible stength. I had to defend myself. We struggled and she fell. It was an accident.'

'Accident or no you now had a new dilemma,' Faro continued relentlessly. 'How to hide the body until Kate's murder was accomplished. Was that when you remembered the frozen loch? You could take her body there and put it at the far end of the loch where the ice was thinner, where it could be broken and the body pushed under the water. Weighted down with stones, she might rot away long before she was found. Another two victims— '

'The woman Rita. She died of shock because she

was asthmatic. She wasn't murdered,' Conan interrupted angrily.

'Precisely. You wanted her to live long enough to confirm that the killer was a woman. Afterwards— ' Faro shrugged. 'If it hadn't been asthma then an overdose of laudanum would have worked as well. You might still have got away with it, and scared Kate into a heart attack by appearing at the kitchen window and writing a threatening note – but your timing was wrong. You were seriously out of luck. Celia's body had been discovered when the loch was being dredged for the drowned student.'

Conan stared at him. 'This is ridiculous. Your case is pretty thin, Inspector. You will have considerable difficulty proving any of this or that I had anything to do with the Glasgow woman's murder.'

'Ah, but there you are quite wrong. As well as Kate, there was one other person you wanted out of the way. Fate seemed to play into your hands when you were returning from visiting your parents in Glasgow and you met Mrs Simms on the Edinburgh train. Unfortunately Rose recognised you talking together.'

'So? I remember the incident. She asked for directions. A mere coincidence— '

'Not quite. Since Mrs Simms was your mistress's mother.'

Conan paled visibly, his knuckles showing white as Faro continued, 'Mrs Simms had never liked you. Until you went through a form of marriage when Dora was pregnant she suspected, quite correctly, that you already had a wife. I don't know what means you used to lure her to Coffin Lane, but you had to keep her with you at all costs until it was dark.'

Faro paused and Conan smiled, no longer seeing any reason to deny it. In fact he sounded rather pleased with himself for the first time. 'I took her for a drive in a carriage around Edinburgh, to see the sights. She liked that, it made her feel important. She was such a bore but I had a hip flask. She always enjoyed a drink. I promised to drive her to Musselburgh.' He shrugged. 'The rest would be easy.'

He laughed. 'This is all conjecture, is it not, Inspector. A game between us. You haven't one shred of proof, not even one witness.'

'Perhaps not. Except that I have been to Glasgow. And I have seen Dora and her baby— '

'What did you tell her about me?'

'Nothing— '

'If you've hurt her, I'll kill you, Faro,' Conan said with low menace.

'I told her nothing. I wanted only to know the truth and saw your child, Conan, your son, who is your image. I would have known even before she showed me the photograph— '

'You've seen him, my son.' Conan smiled.

Still holding Jamie close, he sat back breathlessly. 'My son, a beautiful healthy son, at last. I have no shame about it. Wouldn't any man do the same, be driven to desperation after years with a barren wife? I now have the responsibility of a child. My own flesh and blood. Why should I stay with Kate, who could never give me a son? Besides, she had betrayed me, lied to me about the Tower's hidden gold - there never was a treasure connected with the owl stone—'

He paused and looked round the chapel's bleak stone walls. 'As for being a rich heiress, that was a lie too. There was no fortune to be inherited. Uncle Hedley could have told you. When her father, the laird, died a couple of years ago, he was over the ears in debt. Gambling, speculation, the usual excesses – it runs in the family. Uncle Hedley was better off out of it— '

Faro stared at him. 'Wait a moment. You are admitting that you cold-bloodedly killed Kate because she couldn't give you a child?'

Conan shrugged, unrepentant. 'Let's face it. She was pretty useless as a wife. Had been for years. She had a bad heart and wouldn't have lived more than two or three years at most.'

'And you couldn't wait that long to be free and marry Dora? She seemed the sort of woman who, had you told her, would have waited for you.'

'No, by God. I've waited long enough, wasted enough years already!' Conan shouted. 'I want Dora and my son – now. I won't wait and I hate this place. So I'm going now. And I don't advise you to try and stop me.'

'You won't get very far, Conan,' said Faro sadly.

But Conan's wild eyes, staring, and his trembling told Faro for the first time that he was no longer talking to a sane man. He looked at Jamie and saw the nightmare that was to follow as Conan said gently, 'Oh yes I will. You see, I have Jamie.'

*

'I love Jamie.' He hugged him. 'And if anything happens to me, if anyone threatens me, then his life will be endangered too.'

His eyes gleamed as watching Faro's face he said, 'And you wouldn't want that, the blood of an innocent child, your grandson, on your head. Would you now, Inspector Faro?'

Conan's sudden movement alerted Jamie, who opened his eyes and yawned. As Conan kissed the top of his head, he looked across at Faro, held out his arms and said, 'G'npa here.'

Faro's move towards him was instinctive.

'No. Stay where you are.' Conan made a threatening gesture. 'I am armed and will kill anyone who stands in my way this time.'

And Faro did not doubt him. Not even Jamie would be spared.

'Let me tell you. At first Kate was in it with me, we planned it together, all the way. We'd search for the treasure and once we found it we'd go. Then she got soft-hearted, got fond of her uncle, a useless old man, filthy and disgusting— '

'Did you kill Dr Benjamin to obtain the antiquarian book?' Faro interrupted

'I did not. What do you think I am – a common thief? I wanted to buy it, but he wouldn't sell— '

'So you tried to persuade him by threats and when that didn't work you pushed him downstairs.'

'Of course I didn't,' said Conan heatedly. 'I got around him by telling him that we lived in Solomon's Tower. He said he didn't want to sell the book but that we were most welcome to borrow it to read if we promised to return it. I wished him no harm. The book's around somewhere, but it was a waste of time after all our hopes, utterly useless.'

He regarded Faro triumphantly. 'Uncle Hedley told us that the owl moons clasper was an anagram of Solomon's Tower Chapel. He showed us the secret aperture and told us there was nothing there, nothing but a piece of wood some joker had left at some time. He'd given it to Jamie.'

Jamie looked up at him and smiled trustingly.

Hugging him, Conan said softly, 'We have to go soon.' And to Faro, 'Please don't try to stop us. Jamie is my ticket to freedom. He'll be with me every inch of the way. Try to stop me and you'll kill us both.'

Jamie, fully awake now, looked across at Faro and, wriggling on Conan's knee, stretched out his hand. 'Jamie – go – G'npa.'

Faro was aware of stealthy movement behind him. The door opened and Vince came in.

Conan was unperturbed by his friend's arrival. He looked up smiling, stroking Jamie's curls. 'You've come just in time. Your stepfather's got the wrong end of the stick. Some extraordinary idea that I'm a killer. Does it run in the family, old chap?'

'I think not,' said Vince sadly. 'And I've heard most of what you have confessed— '

'Prove it!' snapped Conan. 'If you can. And now, if you'll be so good, please stand aside. The wee fellow needs some fresh air.'

'Where do you think you're taking Jamie?' demanded Vince.

'Home – my home.'

'And where is that?'

'If you heard it all, you must know. To join Dora and my own son.'

'Then go to your own son, but give me Jamie.'

Conan shook his head sadly. 'Can't do that, old chap. Sorry. You see, Jamie is my ace card, my hostage. Where I go, he goes. As long as I have him like this,' he said, holding him in his arms, 'my freedom is guaranteed.'

'Give him to me!' Vince shouted and started forward.

The hand hidden behind Jamie's back suddenly revealed a small pistol.

'As I warned you, I have this – so stay where you are, both of you. Or else– ' and idly he pointed the pistol at Jamie's head. 'I think you get my message.'

'Conan, give me Jamie and I – we– ' Vince paused to look at Faro who nodded assent. 'We will do whatever you say. We will guarantee your freedom, no police – nothing. The whole incident will be closed.'

'You can go to Glasgow, we'll give you all the time you need,' Faro added. 'We won't notify the authorities, or interfere– '

'In the name of our friendship,' Vince said desperately, 'I beg you – give me Jamie.' His voice ended on a sob, but his passion left Conan untouched.

'Not now, not now. Maybe later – if all goes well, you may indeed see him again. But if not you can be sure that Dora and I will give him a good home, a very good home. We both love children and eventually he will be one of a big happy family, I can assure you. We intend to have lots of children and we'll take excellent care of him. There are excellent opportunities for doctors in Canada. Besides,' he added consolingly, 'I dare say Olivia will give you many more sons. You'll soon get over losing Jamie.'

And looking at his face, serene, unruffled, Faro realised they were trying to reason with a madman who had convinced himself that his fantastic plan to escape was logical. These were the reasonings of an unhinged mind which could end in tragedy, for Conan himself but more important for Vince's son.

As Conan walked to the door, still covering Jamie with his pistol, the child looked across at Vince and Faro and as if aware of some danger, he began to cry, 'Papa – Jamie want Papa.'

'Quiet,' said Conan fiercely, and holding him fast he backed out of the door and clanged it shut behind him.

As Faro and Vince rushed forward, a key turned.

They heard him clattering downstairs, Jamie's wailing cries echoing back to them.

Chapter Twenty-Three

As Jamie's cries died away in the distance both men were already hurling their combined weight against the door, the only exit from the stone chamber. They shouted for help but with scant hope that anyone would hear. Kate was dead. Conan had told them. But where was Sir Hedley?

At last their renewed efforts succeeded and the ancient lock, rusted with damp and disuse in the crumbling stone wall, gave way. They fled downstairs, every moment precious. Sir Hedley did not answer their call and they dared not delay searching for him.

On the road, Vince cursed. The carriage had gone. 'I should have guessed. Brent has orders to let Conan use it at any time.'

'Which way?' gasped Faro.

'He has to head towards the loch where the road widens before he can turn round.'

Thankful that the unmelted banks of snow had made the narrow road impassable, they ran swiftly in the direction the carriage had taken.

'We'll stop him on the way back,' shouted Vince breathlessly. 'Come on.'

Using every last ounce of energy they possessed they ran. Around them the fast-growing dusk had brought a fine drizzle which turned swiftly to sleet, driving horizontally into their faces, but they hardly noticed it.

At last a carriage came towards them. But not Vince's. A man leaned out, alerted by their agitation.

'Going to the accident, are you?'

'What accident?' choked Vince.

'Back at the loch there. Coachman trying to turn on the road. Overturned, I think— '

Chilled with new terror, they waited no longer.

'Jamie, oh my God, Jamie,' Vince cried, and they ran, stumbling, sobbing for breath towards the loch.

The carriage was there, lurched dangerously to one side while a dazed-looking Brent sat at the road-side, holding the horse's reins.

There was no sign of Conan or Jamie.

'Are you hurt?' said Vince.

'No damage done, sir. Just a bit bruised.' Scram-bling to his feet he patted the horse soothingly. 'Jock's fine, too. But the wheel's off. I was just getting my breath back— '

'Where is Dr Pursley?' demanded Faro.

Brent looked around. 'I don't know, sir. I think I must have blacked out for a second. When I came to the doctor and the wee boy weren't inside any longer. Thank God they weren't hurt.'

Darkness was descending rapidly, the heavy clouds already turning from icy sleet to snow. Before them lay the deserted loch with its warning notice: 'Danger. Keep Off. Ice thawing.'

'Over there,' Faro pointed. 'Look, Vince. See them?'

A solitary figure was running across the ice,

heading towards the railway line on the far side of the loch.

Ignoring danger they set off in pursuit, slithering and sliding, Faro clutching Vince's arm to stop himself falling.

'Wait,' he said and looked at his watch. 'The train from Musselburgh – listen!'

They could hear the distant vibrations of its wheels echoing across the stillness.

The ice too began to vibrate. With snow in their faces, hampering visibility, they ran.

Ran . . .

Conan was still forty feet away and they were gaining on him when the ice cracked under him.

An explosion.

They heard him scream as the grey-white waters closed over him.

'Jamie, Jamie,' called Vince, the tears flowing down his face, mingling with the snow. 'My little Jamie.'

'Hold on, lad. We must go carefully,' warned Faro as Vince plunged ahead. 'Easy now.'

They crawled on hands and knees to the edge where Conan had disappeared. There were bubbles on the surface. A movement.

Conan's face and an arm appeared briefly six feet away. He gave gurgling cry for help, and then the waters reclaimed him.

And then Faro saw it, the sight he had most dreaded.

'Look,' said Vince, his voice a hoarse scream.

A few feet away something bobbed up and down in the icy water.

Jamie's bonnet.

Faro seized Vince's arm. 'We'll get him. We can save him, lad, he'll be fine.'

Vince shook his head, and sobbed, 'He can't be fine, Stepfather. You know that. My Jamie's dead. He murdered him.'

'No. *No.* Come on.'

Face down, they edged their way along the ice floe as close as they could get to the drifting bonnet.

But there was little hope in either heart, nothing but the bitterness of bereavement, the grief of unbearable loss.

At that moment they heard a sound.

At first Faro thought it was one of the geese, a wild bird coming in to land on the ice.

'Listen. Listen— '

There it was again.

Not a bird call, but a voice. For them the most beloved small voice in the whole world.

'Papa – Papa— '

Jamie was alive.

'*Pa-pa.*'

'Jamie!'

They looked around, mystified. The voice did not come from the icy water. It came from some twenty feet away, over to their left, clear of the broken ice.

And there was Jamie, unharmed, sitting on an old tree-trunk which the thawed ice had thrown up.

They rushed to him, sobbing with joy.

Vince clutched the child to his heart, held him as if he'd never let go again. And Faro hugged them both, tears coursing down his cheeks.

'Best get back to dry land,' said Faro. 'Come on.'

At the carriage, Brent with a couple of local lads had fixed the wheel, and they bundled Jamie inside.

'Ready to go, sir. All mended. Do we wait for Dr Pursley?'

'No.'

Inside the carriage Jamie protested as Vince ran gentle hands over his arms and legs, while Faro watched anxiously.

Relieved, Vince shook his head. 'He's quite unhurt, thank God.'

'We must get his wet clothes off,' said Faro.

'Wait a moment,' Vince replied in amazement. 'His clothes are quite dry.'

Dry clothes meant that he had never been in the water.

Did this indicate that Conan had had a last-minute change of heart, released him when he knew capture was inevitable?

'Soon have you home,' said Vince consolingly as Jamie began to whimper.

'Naughty C'nan,' he sobbed. 'Not let Jamie go. I scared.'

Faro and Vince exchanged glances.

'Bad C'nan go into water. I scared,' Jamie repeated.

'What happened, precious?' said his father gently.

The child smiled. 'Nice lady lift Jamie' – he pointed – 'up into sky.'

'What lady, darling?'

'Nice lady. In air. All blue— ' He regarded his small clenched fist, held it to his cheek.

'Show Papa, Jamie.'

Smiling brilliantly at them, he opened his hand. In it was a small piece of wood. His toy of the moment, the wood Sir Hedley had given him, all that the niche in the old Templars' Chapel contained.

The secret of the owl moons clasper.

Faro and Vince stared at all the treasure the chapel had ever contained. A fragment of a tree the Templars had brought with them so reverently from Jerusalem, believing it to be from the Sacred Cross where the Son of God hung crucified.

Chapter Twenty-Four

It was the worst Christmas any of them could remember, one they were never to forget.

Kate dead, Conan pulled drowned from the loch, Sir Hedley seriously ill. Obstinately he refused to go to a hospital, grumbled that he was an old man and all he wanted was to die in his own bed surrounded by his beloved cats.

Arrangements were made by Vince, who was looking after him, for a nurse to live in.

There were other grimmer arrangements, but before the funerals of Kate and Conan, came the anguish of breaking such terrible news to the Pursleys.

No police duty in Faro's entire career had ever equalled this. He would spare them the truth, give out the story that authority had accepted. How Conan, distraught over his wife's death, had wandered on to the loch and fallen through the ice.

He would delegate to the Glasgow City Police the distressing task of telling Dora Milthorpe that her bigamous husband had died, leaving her child fatherless. Whatever tact they used, a heartbroken young woman was left to face the world with Conan's son.

After that, silence. There had been enough suffering and Faro was once again unrepentant about concealing the whole truth. But Conan had been right. He had no absolute proof apart from the confession overheard by Vince.

White-faced with shock, William Pursley listened horrified to the terrible news Inspector Faro brought him that Christmas Eve.

He was alone. He would tell Maggie himself when she returned from the Carol Service.

'It is better coming from me,' he said forlornly.

Watching Faro keenly, he said hesitantly, 'There is a story to tell, Inspector. One I never dreamed of telling anyone. I think in all fairness you are the one who should hear it from me. Especially with the poor lad being deranged like that, drowning himself – not able to face life without poor Kate.'

William pulled himself together and spoke with difficulty as he tried to suppress his overwhelming sadness. 'Such a terrible death is also a nightmare coincidence. You see, Conan isn't our child. We fostered him, saved him from drowning. In remarkably similar circumstances which we've tried to put behind us through the years, to forget.'

He smiled sadly. 'We've persuaded ourselves that he was our own bairn, the one we lost so long ago, before we came to Glasgow. His real mother was unmarried, the laird's only sister. They were left orphans and her brother inherited the title when he was fourteen and she was twelve. They were a strange pair, close as twins and he was violently possessive about her.

'I remember her as a pretty, quiet sort of lass, and there were plenty of suitors by the time she was into her teens. There was her fortune too. We must never forget that lure in high society marriages. But although they were short of money, the estate and house neglected, her brother was determined that she should never marry. Any male visitor who looked at her twice was quickly turned away.'

He sighed. 'It reached the stage that they became recluses instead of having the sort of social life young people in their position should have enjoyed. Eventually there were rumours, a maid dismissed, hints that she had seen – well, goings-on between them.

'Rumours ran rife and spread quickly, especially as the young mistress was seen to be pregnant. And who was the father, since no visitors came any more and the poor young lass was virtually her brother's prisoner? Suspicion grew, naturally, that he was responsible for her condition, especially when she walked into the lake and tried to drown herself and the newborn baby.

'You'll remember that I was factor there before I took up the landscape gardening and by the merest chance I was out fishing on the lake. It was dusk and I heard the shouting and the commotion, saw her being pulled out screaming but alive. And alone.

'The laird told me angrily to go about my business when I rowed over to help. I did as I was bid but I can tell you I watched those waters carefully for a sign of the poor drowned bairn. Then as I was mooring the boat near our croft, I heard crying, no louder than the mewing of a kitten. And there was this tiny babe, wrapped in a shawl, lying in the reeds.

'I didn't know what to do, but some instinct told me not to take him back to the castle, but to let

Maggie see him first. We'd just lost our second bairn with convulsions – our wee Conan.'

He paused and, remembering, smiled. 'Maggie just took him in her arms. She still had plenty milk and she said it was a miracle he'd survived. I didn't know what to do but Maggie insisted that we couldn't take the wee soul back, that if his mother didn't succeed in killing him with neglect, then his uncle, who was also his father, would certainly find some means of putting an end to him.'

Pausing, he shook his head. 'Our young laird was no credit to any of us. A scoundrel and a tyrant who had seduced his sister, still a child, and driven her to attempting suicide.

'So we said nothing and passed the bairn off as our Conan. There was no need to worry, the laird never showed the slightest interest in his tenants' lives or their welfare. And he had never been known to visit any of the estate cottages. They hated him for his meanness and neglect so we knew that we could trust them.

'But poor Maggie had nightmares; she was always afraid when we saw him on horseback nearby that instead of riding past, he would stop at our door. And so we decided to leave for the boy's sake. We came to Glasgow and you know the rest of the story.

'We had misgivings at the beginning as to how he would turn out, given his parents, that he might not be – well, normal – but he was a fine sturdy wee chap. A bit irrational and violent sometimes, awful fits of rage, but we reckoned that was on account of his being so brainy. Sharp, clever, right from the start we knew we must give him the best possible chance in life, educate him properly, send him to college.'

He sighed deeply. 'I can scarce believe we'll never see our lad again. Life's cruel sometimes. Taking our poor Kate with the influenza, poor sweet lass. We often wondered whether they were happy together, after he took it so badly that she couldn't have a bairn. But we were wrong. He must have loved her so much, didn't want to go on without her.'

Faro said nothing, he had no more condolences left.

William sighed again. 'This will break his poor mother's heart.'

Before he left, Faro had some questions that urgently needed answers. 'What happened to his real mother? Did you ever hear?'

'We never saw her again. We heard that the laird had sent her to friends in Italy hoping for a complete rest and recovery, and that she had unfortunately died in a cholera epidemic.'

'What was his mother's name?'

'Celia. Lady Celia Belathmont.'

And so the wheel had turned full circle, Faro thought, as the train carried him back to Edinburgh. By some hideous stroke of fate, with all the inevitability of Greek tragedy, after Celia walked into the lake to drown her baby son, retribution had waited thirty-five years, and Conan Pursley would never know that the patient he had cherished and finally murdered was his own mother.

*

As for Faro, he could never forgive himself that he had not interpreted the clues earlier.

'I had it all there, and I think I just refused to recognise what I was seeing, because I liked and respected Conan too much,' he told Vince. 'He was a grand person, a caring doctor and I would have fought anyone who tried to discredit him.'

'I know,' said Vince. 'I feel as if I've lost a brother. I don't think I'll ever have as good a doctor or a friend that close again. I shall always blame his terrible inheritance, that perhaps it was not all his own fault. Maybe we'll have scientific proof some day that he was as mentally disturbed as many of his patients. Lady Celia, his poor mother – if she had known that it was her own son she was besotted with. Dear God. What a frightful end.'

Watching as Vince poured another dram, Faro said: 'I was completely off on the wrong track at the beginning. I suspected that Miss Errington was in it somehow and that she was hiding Molly's killer.'

'There was that one patent slipper, planted, I suppose, by him to start us thinking that the killer was a woman,' said Vince.

'I did give that a fleeting thought. It was rather too pat, somehow. But it was the pantomime that set me on the right road. Seeing Angus in a poke bonnet and some remarks of the women in the row alongside me that he looked exactly like a girl. And that clinched it. I knew that the killer was a man pretending to be Conan's escaped patient.

'I had to go through all the people who knew about the missing Celia and I was left with our family – who I could dismiss – and Sir Hedley and Angus

Spens. Remembering Angus' ghoulish delight in sudden death and corpses, I panicked.

'What, I thought, if he's our killer? How am I to arrest the superintendent's son? What a dilemma that would be.

'Then there was Kate. I considered the possibility that it might be Kate herself and that she'd written the note, especially when I realised the writing was by the same hand as the capital letters on the drawing of the owl moons clasper. I should have got that earlier too, the clasper is such an unusual name for a brooch.'

'Perhaps not for an antique brooch.' said Vince. 'They used words odd-sounding to Lowland ears in the Gaelic translations.'

'Of course, once Celia's body was discovered in the loch I knew that she could not possibly have written the note or have been the woman who almost scared Kate to death. But I did think it odd that Conan – an experienced doctor – was ready to accept a corpse that had been in the water several days as one newly drowned.'

Faro sighed. 'I believe that was the moment I began – most reluctantly – to suspect him.'

'I must confess I suspected Kate – that she'd invented the whole story,' said Vince. 'Although she was the last one I would ever have thought capable of violence of any kind. Such exertion as wielding a knife and stabbing anyone would undoubtedly have brought on a massive heart attack. She would have died before they hit the ground.'

'You're right, and the other clue that declared her innocent was when she told us that Nero hadn't barked a warning and that he raised the roof at the approach of strangers. That was very significant; if a dog doesn't bark then he recognises an intruder as someone who is familiar with the house, someone he knows.'

'At least Nero has come out of it pretty well,' said Vince. 'Did I hear you saying that the City Police were taking him over? Did you arrange that?'

'I did. We need tracking dogs occasionally and big fierce dogs are as good as any constable on the beat. They terrify casual lawbreakers and even innocent folk, come to think of it.'

There was one more surprise in store.

Vince's stony attitude to Sir Hedley melted after having nursed him successfully through pneumonia.

There had been so much bitterness and hatred and he felt he had reason to be grateful to Sir Hedley for entrusting to wee Jamie a piece of wood that Vince would always believe had worked a miracle.

'What about that?' asked Faro.

Vince smiled. 'He has lost interest in it, like all small children. I put it back where it belonged behind the cross in the chapel when I was visiting Sir Hedley.' He shrugged. 'It might be coincidence, but that is one question we are never likely to have answered.'

Walking with Jamie one Sunday afternoon, picking snowdrops to give to his mama on Arthur's Seat, Faro looked down at Solomon's Tower.

A shambling figure was beckoning them from the back door.

Jamie was all eagerness. A toy horse, sadly lacking in paint and mane, who had seen many previous owners, was thrust into his hand.

Jamie beamed. 'Love horsies.'

'Come away in, sir, won't you.'

Faro could hardly refuse and they followed him down the corridor into a room whose grandeur would quickly fade, with curtains torn and upholstery mangled by cat's claws now Kate's restraining presence was gone.

'Do sit down. Smoke? Take a pipe with me.'

Seated, with Jamie on the none too clean floor dividing his attention between the horse and one of the disdainful cats, Sir Hedley said, 'Been looking out for you. Your lad has been good to me. Saved my life. Hadn't much interest in keeping it – after all that happened. Kate dead, Conan drowned. Sorry business. Would have gone willingly to my Maker but for young Vince and the wee lad here.'

Pausing, he leaned over and ruffled Jamie's curls as he wheeled the toy horse past his chair. 'Both remind me of my young days, see.' He frowned. 'Your lad is the image of someone I knew long ago, when I used to shoot over at the Finzeans' place.'

He shrugged and said apologetically, 'Delirious dreams from long ago, but it all came back, y'know, especially when I thought I was a goner. I expect you know from poor Kate that my family were a rum lot. I was glad to get away. Never regretted it. The Tower belonged on my mother's side. Nice and peaceful, no one to quarrel with. Only the cats. But I was telling you about the shoot and this girl.'

'Girl?'

'Did I not say that? The one your lad reminds me of. Just a servant lass she was, but I was head over heels about her. Even asked her to marry me. She turned me down, said she wasn't good enough to be a laird's wife.'

He gave a hoarse, barking laugh. 'Can't say I blame her. Old enough even then to be her father. Eighteen she said she was, but she seemed like a child to me. Didn't intend taking no for an answer, though. Intended coming back at Christmas, persuading her to change her mind.'

He paused, looking out of the window, remembering. 'Sent to India instead. But I never forgot. Next time I was at Finzeans' place, heard she'd left, gone to Edinburgh. Bitterly disappointed, decided I'd had enough of the East, the wine, women and song. So I came to Edinburgh to look for her. Too late though, she had married someone else. Young chap living here.'

He shrugged, his face sad. He looked around the room as if recognising its shortcomings for the first time. 'Just as well, I would have made a poor husband.' Again he paused, and gave Faro a questioning glance from under beetling brows.

Faro felt that favourable comment was expected of him and murmured, 'Nonsense, sir, I'm sure you would have found happiness in the married state.'

Sir Hedley brightened visibly. 'You think so? Well, the way it worked out, she was to be my one and only, y'know. Never loved again. Never wanted anyone else but her all my life,' he added sadly. And then with a frown. 'What was I on about?'

Faro smiled vaguely. 'Your early days, sir.'

'No, that wasn't it. Your son Vince. Can't get him out of my mind. Never could all these years, never knew why. Only lately when he's been looking after me, y'know, once I thought it was her – come back to me. He's her very image – this girl – the one I fell madly in love with. I remember her name. Elizabeth. Elizabeth,' he repeated and laughed. 'Elizabeth. Fine feathers for a skivvy. The other servants called her Lizzie.'

He shook his head. 'But your lad Vince. When he sat with me that night until the fever broke, I could have sworn it was my Lizzie come back to me again.'

Faro was never quite sure how he got home. Once in his study, he closed the door, and laying down his head, he gave vent for the first time to the emotions that swept over him.

His own sweet Lizzie. Fourteen years old, she had told him, with no knowledge of sex, terrified by this older man's ardent advances, fighting him off and failing, then believing that Vince was the child of rape. But in truth he was the love child of a middle-aged man who loved her and had offered her honourable marriage, had gone back to find her and in desperation had moved to Edinburgh to try and find her again.

It didn't matter to Faro that his own marriage had been built on that misunderstanding. He forgave her his own betrayal. Perhaps she believed that if she did not protest her innocence, no respectable man would marry her and Vince would be fatherless. She had lied not only for her son's sake but because she loved him, Jeremy Faro, and was terrified at the thought of losing him.

There was no man living surely who could not forgive such a motive.

What was hardest of all to accept was that Vince's character had been moulded by his mother's protestations of rape, his outlook warped by the wrongful belief of his nativity. His hatred of the society which had betrayed his mother had extended to the unknown man who had fathered him.

And by some strange instinct, that man had become personified in Sir Hedley Marsh.

How would Vince now come to terms with his real father's identity? Was this yet another secret Faro would have to lock away in his own heart and carry to the grave?

Giving it careful consideration, he decided to do nothing until he had come to terms with his own emotions, the dramatic shattering of the foundation of his own marriage.

Enough damage had been done, too many lives lay bruised and broken around him, too many illusions lost for ever. He thought of them all and, remembering the old adage that sorrows could not cross water, he decided to point out to superintendent Spens that he deserved a long holiday.

And tomorrow he would buy a ticket to Ireland.

Author's Note

Imogen Crowe appears in *The Bull Slayers* (Macmillan 1995) and *Murder by Appointment* (Macmillan 1996).

Faro's earlier cases referred to: p.105 *Blood Line*; p.172 *Enter Second Murderer* (included in *Inspector Faro and the Edinburgh Mysteries*, Pan Books 1994); p.49 *The Evil That Men Do* (included in *Inspector Faro's Casebook*, Pan Books 1996); p.119 *The Missing Duchess* (Macmillan 1994).